Mary Lou's Brew

Jennifer Craig

Copyright © 2014 by Jennifer Craig
First Edition – July 2014

ISBN
978-1-4602-4483-8 (Hardcover)
978-1-4602-4484-5 (Paperback)
978-1-4602-4485-2 (eBook)

All rights reserved.

No part of this publication may be reproduced in any form, or by any means, electronic or mechanical, including photocopying, recording, or any information browsing, storage, or retrieval system, without permission in writing from the publisher.

Produced by:

FriesenPress

Suite 300 – 852 Fort Street
Victoria, BC, Canada V8W 1H8

www.friesenpress.com

Distributed to the trade by The Ingram Book Company

Also by Jennifer Craig.

Yes Sister, No Sister: a Leeds Nurse in the 1950s. Breedon Books, 2002.

Yes Sister, No Sister: My Life as a Trainee Nurse in 1950s Yorkshire. Ebury Press, 2010

Jabs, Jenner & Juggernauts: a Look at Vaccination. Impact Investigative Media Productions, 2009

For my grandchildren: Sam, Max, Oliver, Benjamin and Amelia

Acknowledgements

Mary Lou's Brew started as a short story years ago. Then Harry Potter came along and Mary Lou was exiled to a dark cupboard. She emerged once or twice, but it is only in the last couple of years that she demanded to be heard and I paid her attention.

Writers cannot write seriously without the help of many others. My grateful thanks go to:

- My brilliant and insightful writing group: Vangie Bergum, Sarah Butler, Anne deGrace, Rita Moir, and Verna Relkoff. Former members, who also helped with this story, include Susan Andrews Grace, Joyce MacDonald, Antonia Banyard and Kristene Perron.
- Luanne Armstrong, who reviewed an early draft of this story and helped me on my way.
- Tony Rice, my little brother, who quickly latched on to the quirkiness and provided me with ideas for Herman's gadget.
- Charlotte Cole, Editorial Consultant, London, UK.
- Morty Mint of Mint Literary Agency, Nelson, BC.

Warning

Mary Lou's Brew is a satire of a university and is not meant to be taken seriously. So when you come across words like "animopo-morphosis" and "tetra-metra-pseudo-petra" recognize they are made-up words. In Academia, it is frequently the case that you don't know what the faculty are talking about so you just have to shrug and carry on. Readers are expected to do just that.

1

The B.C. Protector's headline, STUDENT SOPHIST FLIES OFF HER HANDLE, met Aurelia B. Virgo's eye the moment she sat at her desk. As Dean of the Academy of Sophists, she was particularly interested in the newspaper's story.

> A second-year student in Sophistry at the University for Bewildered Citizens, crashed her low-emission propellant right into the graduation procession on Friday, toppling the chancellor and causing a dent in the ceremonial copper orb. Sophists have designed a unique form of transportation that they hope will eventually become public but that, at present, can only be used by Sophists as they are the only ones who can incant the necessary affirmation.
>
> The student, Mary Lou Faar, was unhurt but apologetic. "My affirmations aren't strong enough," she said. "I can't focus properly."
>
> Contemporary Sophistry, with a long tradition rooted in ancient Greek culture, and as taught in the Academy, contributes greatly to the whole of humankind, a spokesperson said. Its practices are similar to witchcraft but are rooted in science. Witchcraft broke away from Sophistry in the fifteenth century to form its own sect, and bases its practices on artifice.

The dean closed her eyes and groaned. "Great Logos, who leaked this?"
A knock on her door announced Professor Henrietta Burghul, who marched in waving the newspaper. "Have you seen this?" she demanded.
"Someone, probably Herman, made sure I did," the dean said.

Henrietta gathered her hole-ridden, black gown around her and flung herself onto the chair opposite the desk. "We really have to do something about Mary Lou. She's a disaster. This sort of thing can't go on. Why was she ever promoted into second year?"

The dean leaned back. "She scraped through the exams, that's why. And," she raised her eyes upwards, "her family have been generous in their endowments. Not only that, the Farrs are well known in the heterodoxic world. We can't expel their daughter."

Henrietta, a full professor and confidante, stared at her friend. "Can't we persuade her to take up another career? You know her heart isn't in Sophistry."

"I'm more concerned about who contacted the press." The dean leaned forward to rest her elbows on the desk. "I suspect it was Administration in yet another move to get rid of us. In fact, I've been summoned to the Vice-President's office at," she glanced at her watch, "ten." She stood up. "I better go. But I'll put Mary Lou on the agenda for our next faculty meeting. Maybe someone will come up with a solution."

Dr. Barry Cade, the Vice-President to whom the dean of the Academy of Sophists was responsible, had only been in the university for a few months. She had disliked him on sight; his grey flannels, white shirt, striped tie, navy blazer, polished black laced shoes, and his air of confidence made her want to reach for her talisperson. She had managed, so far, to refrain.

From his first day in office, he had made it clear he had no time for Sophists, despite the dean's attempts to explain their history and curriculum, and why her school belonged in a university. As soon as the dean tried to clarify the practice of Sophistry to him, he would roll his eyes and tell her she and her faculty belonged in a coven, not in a university.

He was sitting at his over-large desk when she arrived, but stood up and waved *The B.C Protector* at her. "This will not do. We can't have the whole world knowing this university pays teachers to promote such nonsense."

The dean's voice was calm and composed. "The general public is very interested in low-emission propellants. The reduction in greenhouse gases is a major goal," she said. "Of course, in the development phase there are bound to be setbacks. Anyone with any sense can see that."

He sat down again, but she moved to one side of him and continued to stand so that he had to twist his neck to look up at her.

"You are always very proud of the research funds you bring in," he began. "Could you give me one example of research undertaken by your school last year that has contributed to the welfare of the community?"

"Yes, if you will do the same for the School of Social Work." The dean's eyes narrowed as she moved round the desk to face him. "I have sent you papers that explain what Sophistry is and how we practice it. I am not here to waste my time repeating myself. My student's mistake was unfortunate, but so was that of the medical student who sewed up a woman's rectum along with the perineum after childbirth."

Cade's face blanched. "How did you know about that?"

The dean gave him her most malicious smile. "When is the court case coming up?"

"Yes, well, accidents do happen when students are learning." Cade's tone was less combative.

"Exactly," the dean said.

The VP leaned back to look up at the still-standing dean. "Won't you sit down?"

The dean pulled up a chair and sat to face him across his desk. Her dark eyes gleamed as she prepared for the expected battle.

"I didn't ask you here to discuss your, er, aerobatic student, but to inform you that the annexes are to be demolished."

The annexes were six ancient wooden huts, similar to army barracks, known as Annexes A through F, scattered across the campus and allocated to the schools least favoured by the Administration. Of these, four were used by the Academy of Sophistry, one by Psychology's overspill, and one by the Institute for Semiotic Studies.

"As you know, they are long past their best before date, and now there's a question of safety." Cade stopped and stared inquiringly at the dean.

"Yes," she said, "do go on."

"The problem is," he pursed his lips and nodded his head slowly; "the problem is that we are not sure where we can house you."

So that's it, the dean thought. They want to get rid of us by removing our space, such as it is. Her regular requests for a new building, or at least a floor in a new building, had always been met with promises but no action. She waited for what he would say next.

"Yes, space is a major problem. There are many competing demands as student enrolment increases and facilities cannot meet the demands placed upon them."

The dean's silence seemed to unsettle him. He wriggled uncomfortably before saying, "The only space we can come up with for you is at Graves."

The dean simply stared at him. Graves was a satellite building miles from the main university that was used for post-graduate studies, Continuing Education, summer schools, and other programs not requiring university resources. It had been built on a former graveyard and although the bodies had been moved to consecrated ground elsewhere, it was still known as 'Graves.'

"Yes. Graves has modern classrooms and offices and should suit you very well," the VP said. "Yes, you should be comfortably housed there."

"Out of the question," the dean said.

After a silence, the VP fiddled with his paper knife and said, "Why? You have always complained about how scattered you are and at Graves you would all be together."

"What about our lab?"

The Academy of Sophistry had a decent laboratory; not thanks to the university but to a thaumaturgist who had donated it on behalf of his daughter who had been left speaking only Zulu due to an unfortunate error in an experiment she conducted as part of her doctoral thesis. Despite intensive efforts by several language experts and the interventions of many senior Sophists, she could not learn another language. As the university demanded a dissertation written in English, she was only allowed to graduate because the dean had persuaded the committee to accept a translation. The student had moved to Kwa-Zulu Natal, South Africa, and her father, in gratitude for his daughter's graduation, had funded a laboratory.

"Yes, that is a problem," the VP acknowledged. "But your propellants do allow your students rapid transportation."

"You expect my students to cross the city every time they want to use the lab?" The dean lips tightened. "Out of the question." She stood up to leave. "Think again."

Cade stood too. "I will try to delay the demolition until a better solution is found, but I can't offer much hope. You must be prepared to move at the end of this academic year."

He stood as if his desk was a protective shield and the dean realised he was frightened of her. So he should be, she thought. She rubbed her talisperson and focused on his crotch. I hope he goes all day with his fly open before he finds his broken zipper, she thought as she marched out of his office.

One of the dean's habits, and one she had tried to quell in her youth, was to mutter out loud. Anyone who knew her well and who saw her striding, black gown swinging, head down muttering, would hastily retreat, so after seeing the VP, she met no one. "That perennial idiot, that supreme prick, that homo non-erectus. May the fleas of a thousand warthogs infest his pubes. If I don't do something about him he's going to spoil my chances of ending my career in glory by getting on the Great Sophist Council. I must make sure nothing goes wrong and the school flourishes this year."

2

Still writhing from the humiliation of crashing her propellant into the academic procession, Mary Lou wandered in a meadow belonging to the Faculty of Agriculture, well away from the main campus, determined to practice on her propellant. Instead of engaging in warm-up exercises, she had propped the idle propellant against a weeping willow tree and had thrown over it the short purple gown that undergraduate Sophists wore in school or when practicing sophistry. She glared at them in disgust.

Mary Lou knew she'd been born into the wrong family. Her parents, grandparents and relatives as far back as anyone could remember were, or had been, Sophist scientists or thaumaturgists – workers of wonders or miracles. The expectation that Mary Lou would follow in the footsteps of her mother, an eminent member of the Group of Eight, was quickly dampened after Mary Lou's first exam results. To join the Group of Eight, the Sophist had to demonstrate a transfocal score of at least 99.24, a rapid response to malign influences, and exceptional somatic senses. Mary Lou showed no promise in any of these areas, and her TF score was a pathetic 33.9.

She had never wanted to participate in the family rites and had done so only through a sense of duty. Even at five years old she was frightened by the ceremony of her mother dancing round the table bearing their All Soul's dinner of braised eel and dumplings on a huge silver platter. It was the eels that scared her: their glassy eyes, their white tubular bodies, and their sardonic grins gave her the creeps.

Then, when her father addressed the seafood dumplings by reciting a poem by the ancient Bard of Yak, she wanted to cry. She had been made to memorize the poem too; how did it go?

Fairy fawn and honest doughface
Great monarch of the dumpling race

Above the eels you take your place
Shrimp, prawn and crabmeat.

Maybe she hadn't got the first line right – she couldn't remember. But she could recall, in vivid detail, her abhorrence as she pierced a slice of eel with her fork and tried to put it in her mouth without gagging. Her mother watched her struggle and, in a moment of rare compassion, allowed Mary Lou to forgo the eel. After all, it was expensive: why waste it on an undeveloped palate?

Mary Lou refused to play with the science kits she was always given for her birthday. She preferred books. Her favourite author was Beatrix Potter, and in Mary Lou's imaginary world, animals wore clothes and danced and got into mischief. She kept an ant colony, ruled by Queen Zoola, that she grew in a glass case and that she would watch for hours. As the worker ants scurried about, she imagined that each wore a hard hat and was dressed in worker's coveralls with tools hanging from the loops. Queen Zoola ruled over them with a kind but firm discipline.

Now, standing in the meadow, Mary Lou watched an anthill, entranced by the constant movement that might seem purposeless to the uninitiated but that she knew was carefully orchestrated by their queen. Ants: so active, minding their own business and working for the common good. They didn't go off to disrupt other creatures' lives like she did. She was supposed to collect frogs' legs for her next lab but the thought sickened her. "I won't do it," she said to the ants. "I just won't do it."

Mary Lou walked disconsolately back to the weeping willow to put her gown on over her jeans and sweatshirt. Then she began the exercises she had been taught to do to help her raise her TF high enough to levitate the propellant. Facing the river and with her mouth wide open, she filled her lungs and let out a prolonged "Voo-o-oom." After three increasingly prolonged Vooms, she switched to the Hexatonical Voom. Performing a Hexatonical Voom in class had earned her an unexpected A, so she engaged in the exercise with enthusiasm. Her "Voom" rose up the scale of F-sharp, hung on the highest note for a moment, and then slowly descended.

After three Hexatonical Vooms she picked up her propellant. "Now come on, blast you," she said, giving it a shake. "Do as I tell you." She rolled it to a level spot, retracted its one wheel, lowered the pedals, and sat on the seat with her feet on the ground. Her eyes fixed on a pile of cow dung as she tried to concentrate.

In her mind she could hear her teacher tell her to breathe. "Deep breath in, hold it, then out with three whooshes. Focus. Again." After three breaths her focus on the cow dung drifted to wondering which cow had made it, how green grass turned into dark, almost-black poop, and why it wasn't solid, like horses. After all, horses ate much the same as cows, didn't they? No, horses ate hay as well. Did cows eat hay?

Shaking herself with annoyance, Mary Lou made herself breathe again and after six breaths she intoned the first chanting aff she had ever composed:

Up in the air like a swift dipsy-doodle,
My propellant will fly like a volatile noodle.

Her teacher thought it was childish but Mary Lou couldn't think of anything else. "It's something I can remember," she had protested, so she was allowed to use it.

Propellants for Sophists began as a form of scooter fuelled by gasoline and reliant on a spark plug to start. Once in motion, and based on early levitation research, they could be made to skim the ground and thus be ridden over rough terrain and avoid highways. Over the years they had developed into what Sophists proudly termed 'low-emission' propellants, as they did not rely on gasoline or engines to start. The latest version resembled a bicycle in that it had a seat and pedals, but there the likeness ended. A hollow, megaloid tube about five feet long and wide enough for a mechanic to insert his arm, formed its basic structure, on which the seat, a handle, and pedals were mounted. There were no chains or brakes, and there was only one small wheel that allowed the user to roll it.

Its major mechanism, its levitation forsometer, operated inside the tube. To the uninformed it looked like a fan, but rather than blow air, it altered the Casimir Force so that upon receiving the energy derived from the rider and her affirmation, the machine would rise from the ground.

The tube widened slightly at the front and more so at the back. A cluster of rubber flanges, screwed on to each side of the front, stuck out like embryonic wings. At the back, larger flanges projected from the end of the tube and the whole machine looked like something da Vinci had designed during a nightmare.

At rest, the flanges lay in heaps, like a cleaning mop, but when the machine had risen by an affirmation chant that activated the levitation forsometer, and once pedalling began, they opened up to direct airflow derived from the troposphere. Pedalling quickly would lift the machine higher, the height depending on the experience of the rider and her TF score.

As Mary Lou chanted, she began to pedal. The front flanges opened briefly but then flopped. She chanted again and pedalled harder. The flanges flapped weakly but did not fully open. She never did get the intonation right. "You have to emphasise the 'dipsy,'" her teacher had told her. Mary Lou repeated the chant with a 'dipsy' that made the cows in the meadow look up from their grazing.

The front flanges opened, the propellant lifted with a jerk and then slowly bounced up and down off the ground. Mary Lou pedalled frantically to open the rear flanges. Finally they sprang open and she became airborne. Not very high, but definitely off the ground.

Now, to steer. The handle wasn't a steering wheel and the pedals did nothing but engage the levitation forsometer that her chant had activated, so the only way to direct a course was through concentration. She knew she had to focus hard on her destination, so she fixed her gaze on the distant gate.

The metal gate with a loop to close it did not occupy Mary Lou's full attention for long and she was soon distracted by a bright clump of dandelions. Her pedalling slowed. Quick, she thought, concentrate! Fix on the gate, on the gate—no, not on that cow pat, the gate! Not the cow pat, not the cow pat…

Both sets of flanges flopped, the propellant nose-dived, and Mary Lou continued her forward motion, landing face first in the pile of cow dung.

3

The dean stretched her long legs under the antiquated table at the front of the classroom in Annex B and tracked a fingernail along the initials RB'57, which must have been carved into the wood fifty-three years ago. It wasn't merely the furniture that was old; the room could use a coat of paint, the windows needed cleaning and, unlike the rest of the university, the lights had still not been replaced with halogen bulbs.

Her encounter with the Vice-President had left her depressed when she wanted to be optimistic and encouraging as the leader of the Faculty of Sophists. She looked up as a shaft of dust-laden sunlight fell across the only wall decoration—a large poster that declared the mission of the school.

Academy of Sophistry

<u>Mission Statement</u>

Our goal is to help students acquire relevant knowledge, skills, and attitudes so that they may practice the Heterodoxic Arts in an informed and responsible manner.

The dean sighed; this simple statement had taken a committee nearly three years to prepare.

Quite simply, the Academy of Sophistry trained students in the art of increasing awareness and dynamism in human experience by introducing vitality stimulants. Such stimulants included irritants: the irritations of daily life, those minor setbacks that humans think are due to chance. Chance, the dean thought wryly; they don't realise the master minds who control such happenings are Sophists. The VP had once asked for examples of 'petty irritations,' as he called them, that Sophists could create, so the dean had scribbled him a list:

Examples of Vitality Stimulants

- The elevator stops on every floor in a high-rise and nobody gets on.
- People slice their tongues licking an envelope.
- Laundry contains a tissue that covers everything with lint.
- People open cans of soup and the lids fall in.
- A CEO looks in the mirror three hours and three meetings after lunch, and discovers a piece of parsley stuck to his front tooth.
- People can never put anything back in a box the way it came.

But why should humans need such stimulation? As a student, the dean had won a prize for an essay that answered this question. Her argument ran:

Patience and humility are desirable human qualities.
    Daily irritations teach patience and humility.
    Humans should be subjected to regular stimulation.
    Sophistry creates these vitality stimulants.
    Therefore, Sophistry is necessary for human character development.

Stimulants wake people up, make them take notice, prevent them sliding into apathy. Not only are people ignorant about the cause of their daily aggravations, they do not understand the skill and training required by Sophists who provide them. Yes, Sophistry is indeed a noble calling.

The dean gazed around the shabby classroom with its five rows of worn wooden chairs arranged in a V shape. The four chairs closest to her, with arms and spaciously arranged, were reserved for full professors; the seven chairs behind them were ready for associate professors, and the three full rows at the back were for assistant professors, teaching assistants, and part-time faculty.

Pensively, she watched her colleagues file in and settle down for their monthly meeting. Dressed, as always, in academic gowns and mortarboards, the faculty formed a sea of black. The dean shook her head slightly. Great Logos, nuns gave up their habits over 50 years ago, but her faculty clung on to their medieval scholar gowns, gowns that were rarely laundered, were threadbare, and smelled of the labs; or worse. They not only clung to their gowns, but they wore their mortarboards at every opportunity. But then, she couldn't really blame them; the other faculties all had uniforms, too: pharmacy teachers wore white coats, veterinary faculty wore khaki coats, and psychologists often grew beards and sported a single earring.

Coloured tassels on the mortarboards clearly delineated rank: amber for Assistant Professors, silver for Associates, and gold for full Professors. The dean did not wear a mortarboard. On special occasions, like graduation ceremonies, she wore a floppy, velvet, medieval hat that she had trouble balancing on her mop of curly hair.

The faculty, or Sophists as they preferred to be called, chatted to each other as they waited for the meeting to begin. With their customary rapid hand and head movements and their black garb, they looked more like a bevy of crows than an academic assembly. The only two male members—dressed in jeans and jackets, one a laboratory assistant in the student lab and one the dean's assistant, Herman Dente—sat quietly together at the back. Herman carried a locked notebook for taking notes that he would share later with the dean as 'Observations from the Backside.'

As the dean cleared her throat to indicate she was ready to begin, each Sophist, with the exception of Professor Wanda Inn, took off her mortarboard and placed it on her lap with the flat side uppermost to serve as a writing surface; Wanda, however, sat bolt upright in the front row, staring straight ahead, the board of her cap adding to her considerable height and blocking the view of the people behind her. Shortly after her appointment to the university as a full professor, Wanda had lobbied senior faculty to have mortarboards abolished. She had been soundly defeated. Her response had been to cut out an inverted U shape in the cap of her board and tilt it back so it rested on the bun formed by her long, white, hair. Several of the senior faculty had complained to the dean, who merely replied that Wanda was wearing a mortarboard, as they had dictated, albeit in an unusual fashion.

Henrietta Burghul, late as always, strode in purposefully to take her place on a front row seat. She nodded to the dean before turning to sit down. Then she said loudly, "Octavia, that is *my* chair."

A wrinkled hand emerged from a voluminous sleeve and Professor Octavia Rale patted the adjacent seat. "You can sit here for a change."

Her hand, adorned with sticky pink dots, had first made the dean wonder if she had chicken pox until she discovered that Octavia used the dots to hide her brown age marks. The dean's comment that natural skin blemishes were preferable to something that resembled a toddler's craft effort was ignored.

Henrietta stopped, glared at Octavia, seemed about to speak then thought better of it and, sweeping her scruffy gown around, her sat bolt upright on the indicated chair. The dean had once made the mistake of speaking to her about her unkempt appearance. With considerable dignity,

Henrietta had informed her that her worth lay in her head, not in her gown, and that she should be judged by her scientific achievements, not her apparel.

The meeting agenda was mercifully short:
1. Business arising;
2. Approval of the addition of Sorex cinereus to the affirmation that encourages door-to-door proselytes;
3. The future of Mary Lou Farr;
4. Progress report on low-emission propellants.

Dean Virgo called the meeting to order, confirmed that everyone had read the minutes, and asked if there were any comments. She closed her eyes briefly as Octavia, the oldest Sophist on faculty, began to struggle to her feet by twisting in her chair, turning her back on the dean and clinging onto the chair arm with both hands.

The dean lifted her head sharply as someone in the back row whispered. As the Dean of Sophistry, one of her special qualifications—in addition to administrative experience and expertise in the heterodoxic arts—was exceptional hearing. The young faculty member didn't realise that the dean could hear her when she asked her neighbour, "How long has that weird old fart been here?"

"Logos knows, but you'd think she'd have snuffed it by now."

"She can barely totter, let alone ride a propellant. And have you seen hers? It's held together with pink duct tape."

The dean glared at the whisperers. It was certainly difficult to believe that Octavia had once been the foremost authority on Levitation with a list of publications as long as your arm and many references in the *Citation Index*. Octavia had been the first to reverse the Casimir force, the force that normally causes objects to stick together. Her discovery led to the creation of frictionless machines with moving parts that could levitate. Although the rest of the scientific world had stagnated at this point, Octavia had continued to experiment and eventually managed to levitate larger objects, including propellants.

Although the dean thought that younger faculty should show more respect, it wasn't surprising that they called Octavia Rale weird. Her wrinkled skin, sparse pink-tinted hair, and pink-framed sunglasses with reflective lenses combined with the standard black gown made her look like a liquorice allsort. And why pink sunglasses? Was she a secret tippler? Had she been pickled for years?

Octavia slowly managed the chair and turned around to face the dean who nodded for her to begin. She still held on to her chair, as if she was afraid Henrietta would grab it, when she looked behind her to address the room. Her voice, when she finally spoke, was filled with indignation. "Item Six. Was it not decided that oxamide is too dangerous a chemical for undergraduate students?"

"Yes," the dean said.

"Yet I saw it in their lab when I dropped in to borrow some potassium unguate the other day."

"So you're the one who stole it," an amber tassel shouted. "I'll have you know they couldn't finish their experiment because YOU had the unguate."

Octavia's back stiffened and she turned slowly to see who was speaking from the lower orders. "And their experiment was ... ?"

"Ensuring cream jugs in coffee shops are always empty."

"With unguate?" Octavia shook her head. "Unguate?" she said, and turned back to the dean. "I did not purloin it," she continued in an imperious tone. "In fact, I only needed zero point zero zero seven five grams. I put the rest back immediately." She glared at the back rows and repeated, "Immediately."

To the dean she said, "I needed it for my experiment on ensuring buttered toast always falls on the buttered side." Octavia's voice took on a dreamy tone. "My levitation work has been enormously influential in this study and I shall be able to furnish you with the results as soon as ..."

The dean glanced at her minutes. "Octavia," she said, "there is no Item Six."

Octavia raised her paper close to her pink glasses. "There's an Item Six on my minutes."

Henrietta grabbed Octavia's paper. "Someone has written 1836 in the margin."

"Oh yes," Octavia said. "I was reading Frankinsop's exposition on oxamide. Very interesting. She suggests, because oxamide is mined in the foothills of the Sahara, that ..."

"Yes, yes," the dean said. "I understand your concern. However, if you look at the minutes from the last meeting more carefully it was oxammite we discussed, not oxamide." She glanced at her copy of the minutes. "It does say oxammite here."

"Surely the topic of oxamide is important?" Octavia said.

"Yes it is, Octavia, but not right now," the dean said. "This is a faculty meeting." She looked round the room. "Any other business arising from the minutes?" She noticed that Octavia was about to speak again. "No? Very well. Let us discuss the addition of Sorex cinereus to the proselyte affirmation. Comments?"

The dean groaned inwardly as Ciesta Sands, the only obese Sophist on faculty, laboriously struggled to her feet from an associate professor chair that had been strategically placed with room between its neighbours on either side. The loud, red, hair stripe across Ciesta's head caused the dean to frown. Since winning a huge grant from the National Foundation for Hexonic Research[1], Ciesta had become increasingly outrageous, which was fine, the dean thought, but not this screaming red.

"Why would you add Sorex? Isn't this a case … of fixing something … that ain't broke?" Ciesta asked with a dramatic flinging out of one arm that showed off her ring-laden fingers and revealed a silver lamé shirt under her gown. Her lungs, severely taxed even under resting conditions, only allowed her to speak in short bursts. "The aff … has been working … satisfactorily for years. The number of proselytes … increases annually."

"I beg to differ." Henrietta stood up and turned to Ciesta. "Recent statistics from the University of Lichtenstein—preliminary results from their longitudinal study—show a zero point six five probability of failure when it is used in rainy weather. Sorex cinereus removes this impediment." Henrietta sat down and examined her fingernails.

Not easily silenced, Ciesta persisted. "Is there not … something more readily … attainable that would have … the same effect?"

"Now there's a research project for you, Ciesta," the dean said.

Ciesta's mouth set in a hard line. "I'm already busy … with my progressive studies of … trinamite as a dietary supplement … to increase abdominal tumescence," she said huffily. "Sorex cinereus … is expensive and hard to come by."

"Don't they exhibit cordus elimina when frightened?" an amber tassel asked.

"If you mean they lose their tails, say so," her neighbour said.

"I just did. Are you Latin-deficient?"

The dean raised her hand and said, "Order."

"We could send out a posse of students to frighten the Sorex and then collect their tails," a voice from the back row said. "Make a nice field trip."

"A nice, mice field trip," someone added.

"It's scincus that lose their tails, not Sorex cinereus," a young Sophist said. "It would make a nice, mice field trip if they were mice. But they're not; a scincus is a form of lizard. So it would make a wizard, lizard jaunt."

Ciesta, who was still on her feet, glared at the jokers. Her noisy intake of breath caused Henrietta to glare at her and say, "Question."

The dean gave Henrietta a grateful glance. "All in favour," she said. She counted the raised arms. "Twenty-three. Against?" Ciesta raised her arm. "Carried. Now let us turn to the question of Mary Lou Farr."

---

1   NFXR 56290. Investigation into factors that contribute to the twentieth century decline in hexonic research.

There were 160 undergraduate students in the academy, forty in each of the four years required to earn a Bachelor of Sophistry, a BS. Most problem students were handled by their individual professors, but because Mary Lou had caused so much trouble in her first year, culminating in the crash, the dean hoped for a solution.

"It is the first time in the history of this academy," she said, "that we have had a student as, er, non-nonconforming, as Mary Lou. We have to remember that a nonconformist can be a genius. Unlikely, I admit, but we do have the example of Bedragga[2], who became the most forward thinking Sophist of her time. But, before we consider Mary Lou's inadequacies, does anyone have anything positive to say about her?"

There was long silence before someone from the back spoke. "Which one is Mary Lou?"

"She's in second year. Short black hair. Freckles. Looks more like a Phys Ed student than a Sophist."

"Oh, yes, I remember her. Her work in first year Hexaphronics was good. She designed a very fine talisperson."

"I found her a disaster in the lab. Every time she tried to light her lebes she set it on fire. Or else it wouldn't light."

The teachers sighed and shook their heads. "Perhaps she purchased an inferior brand?"

"No, it's an Athena like all the others. Who hexed it for her?" an amber tassel asked, looking around accusingly.

Wanda stood up and surveyed the room. "I did."

The silence acknowledged that Wanda's transfocal score was higher than any other in the room, second only to the dean, and therefore the hex would be dynamic.

"She does try," the Equipoise teacher said. "But I'm afraid she struggles with the idea that negative forces are necessary. She simply doesn't understand that without a negative force you can't have a positive one."

"No, she hasn't a clue," Prunella Peidmore, a second-year teacher said. "When I asked her to think of a vitality stimulant and how she would design an aff, she suggested things like removing dog smells from cars. Not how to introduce them."

"Apart from crashing into the chancellor, how's her propellant skill coming along?"

"She can start it but then she stops concentrating to admire the scenery."

A thoughtful silence took over before someone said, "I don't know what the Admissions Committee was thinking of when they accepted her in the first place."

"She comes from a long line of Sophists," a member of the Admissions Committee said, "and she scored high on the Sophistry Aptitude Test. Our decision was justified."

"Perhaps her parents' endowment to the school had something to do with it?" an amber tassel remarked. The dean frowned at her.

"Ah, but she did well in Modern Cantus. She thought of quite innovative rhyming affs."

"It's no good composing rhyming affs if you can't use them. What's her TF?"

"I'm afraid her transfocal score is way below average," the Trivium coordinator said. "I've given her many exercises to bring it up. She performs them, yes, but the outcomes are poor. She has the concentration of a three-year-old."

"That sounds like the basis of her problem," the dean said. "Oh dear. It's keeping her from being able to apply her limbic energy. If she never masters affs, she'll never succeed." She looked round the room. "Any suggestions for helping her?"

"I'm not sure she really wants to be a Sophist, so the motivation isn't there," Henrietta said.

The dean raised her hand. "I think we should give her another chance with some extra tutoring. Then if she hasn't improved by the end of this term, we'll have to let her go." She looked around to pick a suitable tutor. There was young Prunella, who was very popular with students but would likely encourage Mary Lou's non-conformity, as she was so scornful of tradition herself. Ciesta? No, her ribald approach to life made her too... Word for not being serious enough? Flippant. Yes, she was too flippant. Henrietta and Wanda were full professors, and asking them to tutor an undergraduate student would be an insult. Octavia was also too senior, but anyway she got so muddled she would confuse Mary Lou. Matilda? Yes, Matilda was conscientious. Too prissy for the dean, but she would make a good tutor for Mary Lou. "Matilda," she said, "would you take her on?"

Matilda deMeow, an Associate Professor with an MHA (Mistress of Heterodoxic Arts), was a respected academic. She had written many papers, the most notable being one on an affirmation to create verruca vulgaris on thumbs, published in *The Lebes*.[3] This timely study had been received enthusiastically by the public because thumb warts, though harmless, greatly impeded their teenagers' ability to text.

---

3   M. deMeo. "A randomized controlled trial of the effect of Thlaspi Arvense on an affirmation to create verruca vulgaris on thumbs." *The Lebes* (506): 202-216, 2005

Matilda glared at the dean. She pursed her lips and hissed, "You know I have a deadline for a grant application." She scanned the room. "And *we* all know how important it is to get grants right now."

"Yes Matilda, but I was thinking that if Mary Lou can't learn from you, then there is no hope for her," the dean said. "She won't take up too much of your time, I'm sure." After a pause, she added, "I'll help her with her TF."

Matilda thought for a moment and replied, "Yes, I will take her on. But," she added, "for one month only. And I will not guarantee her success."

"Thank you," the dean said, and nodded to her. She looked around the room. "Next I want to discuss propellants." She sighed. "There are many design problems, which are holding up production. Comments?"

Matilda said, "At their current stage of development, propellants are extremely difficult to ride. Indeed, even at my level of expertise, I have trouble."

"I know a lot depends on the strength of the aff, but even students with adequate TF scores are having trouble mastering them," Henrietta said.

"I doubt if they'll ever be ready for the public," an amber tassel chipped in. Her neighbours murmured, "True, true."

"I believe the problem lies in the flanges," the dean said. "Currently they are made of rubber, but perhaps some other material...?"

"Who is working on them?" someone asked.

Wanda stood up. Being six feet tall, plus the height of her mortar board, she presented an imposing figure. Normally her wide, smooth-skinned face with its full lips and sparkling eyes made people want to smile, but she could assume a frightening scowl, which she had on as she spoke. "I am the principal investigator, and my lab assistants are testing other materials to make flanges. Currently we're experimenting with Megaleg Tetracarbon."

"Megaleg Tetracarbon is completely unsuitable," a silver tassel said. "Its Dohm ratio is too high for it to interact with xenon. You should try Megaleg Petracarbon."

"Thank you," Wanda said, "but although Megaleg Petracarbon's Dohm ratio is satisfactory, its molecular absorptivity is too reactive." She turned to the dean with a smirk. "We are working on it."

The dean admired Wanda, not only because of her stance on mortarboards, but because of her expertise in electrophrenetic dynamics. With her Jamaican roots and her talisperson made from the tail feathers of the doctor bird, no one messed with Wanda.

The dean said, "Good. If we can master the problem and design a reliable, carbon-free mode of transport, our school will receive such accolades and grants there will be no question of our survival in the university."

The faculty murmured approval.

"Is there any other business?" the dean asked. She saw that Octavia was about to speak so she quickly said, "No? I just want to mention, before I adjourn the meeting, that there's more talk of demolishing the annexes, which will further reduce the space our school is allocated. However, there is no need for concern at present."

The dean drew the meeting to a close without mentioning that unless something dramatic happened soon, they would all be housed in Graves.

4

Dragging the propellant on its one wheel, Mary Lou limped back to her college dorm and to the room she shared with Julie Hyde. Mary Lou always thought that Julie was the ideal future sophist, with her straight black hair, aquiline nose, and heavy-lidded eyes. In contrast, Mary Lou's cheerful face with its freckles and full lips definitely belonged in another profession.

Julie lay on her bed reading but she looked up to say, "Professor deMeow wants to see you."

"Oh geez, what for?" Mary Lou tossed her purple robe on her bed.

"How should I know?" Julie said. "I found a note on the door when I came in." She sat up to stare. Then she snorted. "What the hell have you got on your face? It looks like cow poo."

Mary Lou plonked down on her bed. "I've been practicing on my frigging propellant," she said, "but I still can't steer. I really tried to focus but it headed straight for a cow pat."

"You have to focus on where you want to go." Julie was the top of the class in Propulsion and spoke with authority. "What did you focus on?"

Mary Lou rolled her eyes. "A gate. But it landed me in cow pat near the gate." She laughed. "I better go wash before I see deMeow."

Mary Lou showered, put on her gown and set off for the faculty offices. She couldn't understand why deMeow had sent for her as she was not one of Mary Lou's tutors, and professors simply did not make a habit of arranging one-on-ones with students. None of the students really minded having to approach a professor in a group setting, but deMeow's twitchy nose made close-up encounters with her both distracting and unnerving.

As a graduate student, Matilda deMeow's field of interest had been in the energy emitted by the scut of cunicula. It was well known in sophistry that for most creatures, the tail generates the most energy, but Matilda wondered if this dictum held true for rabbit tails, their scuts. Her work in the lab with standard measuring instruments such as the spectrodynometer proved unenlightening, so she turned to the study of lycanthropy—or shape shifting, as it is popularly known—whereby man is changed into animal form. She reasoned that if she could metamorphosise into a rabbit, or even a part-rabbit, she could study a scut from the inside.

Sophistry was well versed in metamorphosis, and her review of its literature took many weeks. How she achieved rabbithood, not the energy of scuts, became the primary topic of her dissertation, which was just as well as there was no more to be gained from measuring her scut from her gut than from her butt.

All honest scientists discuss their failures as well as their successes, and Matilda had to confess that, while the metamorphosis had proceeded without incident, a full conversion back to normal had been incomplete, and two features of cunicula remained: a twitchy nose, and a scut.

As her nose had been her best feature, Matilda was greatly disturbed by its mesmerizing jerks. Not only that—and this was a fact she kept hidden—the white fluffy scut on her sacrum was intensely itchy, and left her with an almost uncontrollable urge to continually scratch her bum.

Mary Lou knocked on Matilda's door with a trembling hand.

"Ingress," she heard a voice say.

Matilda sat at her desk and leaned back as Mary Lou entered.

"Ah, Mary Lou. Sit down. There are matters I wish to speak to you about. The faculty is concerned about your progress. It seems that you are failing both the theoretical and the practical courses. Would you care to comment?"

Mary Lou sighed. "Second year is harder than I thought."

"What do you find the most difficult?"

Mary Lou stared at the wall and finally said, "Using creatures to make affs."

"But that's what we've done for centuries. I've never heard a student complain before." Matilda moved her glasses to the end of her extraordinarily long pointed nose then leaned forward to stare intently over them at Mary Lou. "Do you really want to be a Sophist? Is it your chosen vocation?"

"All my family assumed that's what I'd be," Mary Lou shifted on her chair, "but I'm not sure. The main thing is, I don't think I can. I can't concentrate enough for one thing, but mainly …" she paused and then burst out, "I simply can't use creatures in experiments. I think it's cruel."

Matilda's nose began to twitch. "You come from a long line of Sophists, I believe," she said. "Have you talked to your family about your reservations?"

Mary Lou wriggled uncomfortably. "No."

Matilda pondered for a minute and then said, "Very well, Mary Lou. I'll tell you what I want you to do. You are to create an imbibing aff with any ingredients you choose. Study in the library. Know the chemical constituents of each ingredient. You may use the lab at any time to test them out, and you can come and see me for advice whenever you like. Then, in one month, you must demonstrate your aff to the faculty."

Mary Lou stared at her. "Oh, thank you. Yes. I shall really try." She tried to sound enthusiastic.

"Also, compose a chanting aff to turn your brew into a hex. Can you do that?"

"Yes, I'm good at chanting affs." Mary Lou stood up.

"Before you go, the dean wishes to see you. She'll help you raise your TF."

Mary Lou's eyes widened. "What? Now?"

"Go to her office and make an appointment." Matilda looked at her own appointment book to indicate the interview was over.

Mary Lou sighed with relief as she left Matilda's office. She still was not sure whether she wanted to continue at the school, and she wondered if she was up to the challenge of creating a new imbibing aff even if it meant not killing the ingredients. On the other hand, if she were to leave, what would she do? She didn't think her parents would condone, or pay for, other training. On one occasion she had mentioned she would like to be a wildlife vet and the idea was met with such scorn she didn't mention it again. She didn't want to quit because she had failed. No, there was nothing else for it but to try to pass this test. If she did well, and graduated, then she could approach her parents about a change.

5

Dean Virgo sat at her desk scraping the inside of her nails with a metal paper knife and thinking of words she enjoyed that could describe Prunella. To keep herself sane, she'd recently started a course in memoir writing, so her mind frequently turned to words and catchy phrases that would allow future readers to participate in her life as Dean of the Academy of Sophists. Unscrupulous; a lovely word. Unscrupulous. Callous. Parsimonious. How they roll over the tongue. Parsimonious is not unscrupulous. Callous, no. Relinquishing all morals to further her ambition does not describe Prunella. Young, yes, ambitious, yes, but not unscrupulous.

Prunella Peidmore, an Assistant Professor, was up for tenure and, although the decision was not hers alone, the dean did not think she would succeed. To save the Promotions Committee the frustrating task of considering Prunella's inadequate record, the dean decided to talk to her and attempt to steer her in another direction.

The dean knew that Prunella was popular with students but not with her colleagues. Students liked her because she designed interesting lessons in which they were involved. Furthermore, she held the quaint notion that if faculty told students what was important to learn, helped them learn, and tested them on what they had learned, that they would succeed. Prunella believed in telling students what was to be on the exam, an idea that had older teachers running to the dean in outrage. The dean had been able to point out that, despite knowing the content of the test, student scores still fell on the same bell curve as usual.

Prunella's colleagues considered her a young upstart who was too keen to criticise their long-held practices. She had once openly scoffed at an examination that Octavia Rale had set because it asked such questions as, 'How many pages are there in Circuta's 1643 exposition on circular, diametric patterns?' and 'What colour is nitro-placto-brocterium?'

Prunella said that such questions encouraged students to memorise trivia instead of encouraging them to think. As much as the dean may have agreed with her, most of her energy had gone to soothing Octavia who was, after all, a senior member of her faculty.

She recalled the scene with a smile: Octavia had arrived in her office fuming so badly that she could not sit down, but flapped her gown backwards and forwards in front of the dean's desk, creating a draught. "That woman," Octavia spluttered, "that woman should be extransmitted. At once. Today."

"Don't you think that's a bit extreme?" the dean said. "Public censure by the Council and the end of her career?"

"But she said—she said I'm a dodo! A young upstart who has the temerity to call me a dodo deserves… As if I've never composed exam questions before. I've done it for years. No one has complained before. I'd like to—"

"Calm down, Octavia. Prunella is up for tenure soon. You sit on the Promotions Committee do you not?"

Octavia's eyes gleamed. She sat down and rubbed her hands. "I do, yes." She said. "Indeed I do."

Now the dean waited for Prunella to arrive for a meeting to discuss her application for tenure. Prunella confidently entered the dean's office and sat down.

"Have a seat, Prunella," the dean said. Prunella flushed slightly. The dean leaned back and looked thoughtful. Then she leaned forward. "I think we need to talk about your application for tenure."

"Oh yes," Prunella said. "I think I've done everything. I'm pretty confident."

The dean frowned. This was going to be more difficult than she had thought. "I'm quite sure there is a place where your talents would be better deployed than here, in a university. Your research record is sadly lacking, I'm afraid. Not quite what the Promotions Committee would like to see."

"But I just won a teaching award," Prunella said.

"You're a good teacher, I'll grant you that, but that isn't important in a university. Obtaining research grants and publishing in reputable journals is vital if you are to survive in an academic setting."

"I have put in for grants," Prunella said. "I'm researching how examination scores of propellant flying correlate with three-dimensional perception."

The dean sighed. "Yes, but you know as well as I do that the funding comes from the Panacean Industry and they're not interested in education."

Prunella crossed her legs. "But surely the major role of a university is to educate students?"

"Oh Prunella, don't be so naïve." The dean stared at Prunella, wishing she would just go away. That assertive stance Prunella adopted, the way she set her shoulders, the way she raised her chin, was beginning to get on her nerves. Surely the woman had clued in to how a university operates by now.

"Are you telling me I won't get tenure?" Prunella asked.

"The decision isn't mine to make. As you know, a committee makes the decisions."

"But you sit on it."

"I chair it. I don't have a vote."

"You do if the committee is split." Prunella thrust out her chin. "If it was split over my tenure, which way would you vote?"

The dean stared at her thoughtfully. "I don't think the question will arise. The committee is usually of one mind."

"But supposing it was split over me," Prunella repeated, "how would you vote?"

"Interesting question." The dean frowned. If she said yes, what would Prunella do when she heard that she'd been refused tenure? For the dean was quite sure the committee of older faculty would reject her application. If she said she would vote no, she would have to put up with the woman's reaction, not just right now but for the rest of the term. "I haven't studied your record well enough to make a decision at this moment," the dean said. "I asked you here to discuss your application and see if you have any plans should it be turned down."

Prunella gave her a humourless smile. "Huh," she grunted.

"I beg your pardon?" The dean thrust her head out with one ear towards Prunella.

"Who sits on the committee?"

"Four senior members of faculty and an ex-officio member from another faculty."

"The dodos, you mean," Prunella said.

"Calling senior faculty dodos does nothing to improve your chances of success." The dean wanted to lie down and close her eyes.

"But they are." Prunella's voice rose. "They haven't had a new idea since the Dark Ages. Once they get tenure they fulminate – no, I mean, vegetate. Decay. Everything has to be done exactly as it was done fifty years ago. Well, things have moved on since then." Prunella thumped the air with her fist. "There is so much we can do with computers, for example. So much. Yet they don't even know how to switch one on. And they don't want to know. That's what gets me. There are so many affs we can make with computer models, and what do the dodos do? Mess with mouse tails in the lab."

The dean clenched her jaw and took the opportunity of a pause in the tirade to say, "Yes Prunella, I can see how your talents are being wasted here and how frustrated you are. That is why I want you to consider your position. Even if you get tenure, things won't change. You will be as frustrated as ever."

Prunella bit her lips and remained silent for a while. "Hmm," she said, "perhaps you're right. I might be better off in a college, where teaching skills are valued."

"Exactly," the dean said. "But only if you don't get tenure, you understand. There is still a chance. I just want you to have a plan in case your application fails."

"Thank you, dean," Prunella said. "But I would still like to know who sits on the committee."

The hint of menace in Prunella's voice shook the dean out of her complacency; the interview had not gone as she planned. "This year it's Matilda, Octavia, Wanda and Ciesta, I believe. But Prunella, any idea of retaliation is not wise," she said. "Remember that senior faculty have had years of experience in affirmations and hexes—years." She paused. "There have been incidents when students or junior faculty have attempted to put hexes on experienced Sophists and they have always ended with disaster for the junior."

"I'll remember that," Prunella said. She stood up to leave.

Except for one incident, the dean thought as she watched Prunella's retreating back. And who are you to give a warning like that? She smiled.

Prunella stomped to her office and slammed the door. She still wasn't sure about the dean's opinion of her, since the dean had successfully evaded her direct questions. But she was obviously not going to get the promotion. Did she really want tenure? It would mean staying in this stuffy place with its out-moded ideas. On the other hand she would be able to teach senior students instead of forever supervising beginners in the lab, and it would allow her to do research in education and show the dodos that they didn't know what they were doing.

Prunella gazed at the elaborate scroll from the Diabolic Pedagogic Institute announcing that she was the Teacher of the Year. Her students had nominated her. She had always glowed with pleasure each time she looked at it, but now she shook her head. A useless piece of paper, signifying nothing. It would have been better if she had concentrated on simple experiments like making people spill coffee on themselves when they were in a hurry, or making chewing gum stick to the sole of shoes. Instead, she had measured the validity and reliability of exam questions. What did it matter if exam questions bore no relationship to the course content? Who cares?

She did not have time to do a significantly trivial experiment that would impress the Promotions Committee, but she wanted to do something, not just passively accept her fate and leave. Logos, if she could only remove the entire senior faculty, or at least the ones who made up the Promotions Committee, then she'd stand a better chance of promotion. If she could convince a new committee that her work in education was as valid and scientific as any done in bio-hexonic sciences, she would stand a chance. A new committee would be more open-minded than the present bunch, the dodos, so set in their ways they had solidified.

Now, who did the dean say was on the Promotions Committee? Octavia, who can barely stand up; Wanda, who can't recognise a good exam question if it slaps her in the face; Matilda the Twitch, who is too timid to think, and Ciesta the Rotund, who thinks everything is funny. And to think they were in a position to decide her future. No way.

She considered the four names and wrote them several times on her pad. Matilda, Ciesta, Octavia, Wanda. How was she to get rid of them?

6

The dean controlled her irritation with Prunella by turning to the pile of letters awaiting her attention. She had just signed the first one, A. B. Virgo, when the secretary announced that the student she wished to see, Mary Lou, was in the office.

The dean sighed. She could postpone the interview, but a glance at her watch informed her that office hours were still open, so she told the secretary to show Mary Lou in.

Mary Lou stood nervously in front of the desk as the dean regarded her. How could you not like the child, the dean thought. So young, so innocent, with her open face and snub nose. She certainly does look out of place among Sophists who value severe features and narrow eyes. "Sit down, Mary Lou. I hear you are not doing too well," she said. "What do you think?"

Mary Lou sat down and gripped her hands. After a pause she blurted out, "I don't think I'm cut out to be a Sophist."

"Why is that?" the dean leaned forward and tried not to look intimidating.

"I can't concentrate enough but my main problem is… is using animal parts." She looked at the dean with wet eyes. "I think it's cruel to use parts of helpless animals, parts they need to live and parts I don't think we need. At least not that much."

"Have you talked to Matilda yet?"

"Yes. She's told me to make an imbibing aff with any ingredients I want," Mary Lou said, "which is great, but then what? I can't concentrate enough to ride a propellant, or do anything for that matter. My TF score is the sh… er, below average."

The dean suppressed a smile. "What exercises do you do? Before riding for example."

"I'm pretty good at Hexatonical Vooms but my focus doesn't last long. I drift off." Mary Lou stopped playing with her fingers and looked at the dean.

"Yes, it is difficult to stay focused, particularly if you have an active mind." The dean remembered how hard she had found it to concentrate on one thing and how impatient her teachers were. Now, she realised, she hardly even thought about it as her focus, when she applied it, automatically went into action even without an aff. "I will show you an exercise. It's easy. It's called the Guyan Mudra. You hold your hands like this."

The dean placed both her forefingers on her thumbs and extended the other fingers straight. Mary Lou followed suit.

"Do this during lectures, for example, do it every time you remember to, and it will help your mind settle." The dean stood up. "Come over here." She moved to the door and opened it. "See. It's unlocked. Now ..." she held her hands in Guyan Mudra for a few seconds as she stared at the door lock, then she rubbed her talisperson. "Now try the door."

Mary Lou twisted the door knob. "It's locked," she said. "How did you do that?'

"Focus on what you want to do as you chant an aff and activate your talisperson to apply the hex," the dean said. "Now you try to unlock it."

"But you didn't chant an aff?"

"No. When you're an expert you can leave that bit out. But it does help, at first."

With a frown of concentration Mary Lou held her hands as the dean had shown her and stared at the door knob. After a few moments she chanted,

If this door I can unlock,
the dean will get an awesome shock.

Then she rubbed her talisperson and willed the door to unlock. She tried the handle. It opened.

Delighted, she turned to the dean with a huge grin. "It worked!"

"See, you can do it," the dean said. "Now, I want you to keep practicing the Guyan Mudra and the use of your talisperson. It will soon become second nature."

"Oh thank you," Mary Lou said, as she practically skipped away.

The dean smiled. Would the child realise it was not she who had put the hex on to unlock the door? But she thinks she did and that encouragement is what's important.

The dean had nearly finished clearing her In basket when she was interrupted by Herman, her personal assistant. He quietly entered her office in his usual obsequious way and stood in front of her desk swaying from side to side.

"What is it?" she said. "I'm trying to finish a writing assignment."

Herman said nothing. She looked up to see his sagging shoulders and drooping mouth. He was definitely weird; no, not weird, goofy. But why? Was it his widow's peak? No, those were greatly admired in the heterodoxic arts world. The intelligent, bright brown eyes peering out from under protruding brow ridges gave him a rather distinguished visage, but he didn't command respect. Why not? What was it about him that made him over-looked? He had a rather pronounced overbite, but that was only noticeable when he smiled. It couldn't be his blonde dreadlocks; such a hairstyle was well accepted, particularly on campus. It must be his posture. He was tall and as gangly as a teen-ager and, like a teen-ager, he was clumsy and always falling over things, as though he still couldn't control his limbs. But his fine motor coordination was acute: he was a whiz at electronics, and could manipulate the tiniest screws and parts.

The dean sighed. "What's the matter, Herman?"

"I can't get the jammer data analysed."

"Can't it wait until we're in the lab? I have to finish this."

"We're not in the lab until Saturday." Herman shuffled his feet and put on the spaniel expression that he had perfected.

"Herman," the dean said firmly, "on Saturday I will give you my undivided attention. Until then I'm busy." She picked up her pen and turned her attention to her paper.

Herman swayed in the way that drove the dean to distraction. She put her pen down and looked up at him with a resigned expression. She knew from experience that she would never have any peace until she had attended to him. "All right, what's the problem?"

Herman smiled, exposing a row of beautiful, white teeth marred only by the overbite. He produced a notebook he had been holding behind his back and laid it down in front of the dean. "This is the formula I've been working on, but there's something wrong."

Herman was trying to construct a device—a jammer—much like a garage opener, that, when aimed at an engine, switched it off. He figured he would find a huge market for it in people who are irritated by sea-doos, ski-doos, tailgating cars, and the like. Although Herman was skilled in electronics, the jammer needed a hex and, as he had not taken a degree in thaumaturgy, this is where the dean came in.

Although this project was contrary to the goal of Sophistry, which was to increase irritation, the school needed the income derived from its research and so, like propellants, it encouraged such endeavours. The dean thought Herman's jammer was interesting and could lead to other more suitable projects such as switching off people's computers in the middle of PowerPoint presentations.

"Herman, you know that I don't know much about electronics. You have to have got the thing working before I can make it do what you want it to do."

As she studied his chart he stood, pulling his black tee shirt down as far as it would stretch so that it outlined his thin chest. She stared at the formulae on the chart trying to make sense of it.

Beam wavelength (nano m)	Beam colour	JIM beam* (thurbligs)	Radius (yards)	JIU*
1	red	7.3803845	10	4
0.25	orange	7.8944905	25	1
0.75	yellow	6.2481214	50	0.444444
0.5	green	3.7215301	75	0.25
0.75	blue	9.2989617	100	0.16
0.25	violet	8.9436356	125	0.111111
1	indigo	2.0518933	150	0.081633

*JIM Beam = jamming intensity magnification in thurbligs
*JIU (Jamming Intensity Unit) = inversely proportional to the square of the distance from home.

Herman shifted his weight from foot to foot and then said, "the JIU is the most important factor. When I've got that right I'll have to spend weeks working out over 700 permutations to find the right ones. But if there's an error at this stage, then there'll be an error in all the permutations."

"And the JIU is...?"

"The Jamming Intensity Unit. It's inversely proportional—"

"Yes, it says it right here." The dean pointed at the paper. "But what does it *mean*?"

Herman paused for a moment so that the dean wondered if she had asked a really stupid question. "It doesn't mean my home of course," he said. "Home is where the jammer is operating."

"Got that," the dean said, "but what does the reading mean? What does it convey?"

"It means how well the jammer performed. How close to the bullseye, if you like; how close to success."

"Oh," the dean said. She studied the chart again. "And the JIM Beam?"

"That's the intensity of the beam—its magnification. The beam column alone is its wavelength. The beam, of course, is what turns off the switch."

"I see." The dean didn't see but she did want to encourage Herman. Then she said, "Why the colour?"

"That's the colour of the beam. It follows the colours of the rainbow." Herman began to run his fingers through his hair. "I don't understand it. The design is unusual, yes, but…" He cleared his throat, "It's brilliant. No one has done anything like this before. You'll get a fine paper out of it, dean."

"Richard of York gained battles in vain," the dean said.

"What?" Herman's eyes widened.

"The colours of the rainbow," the dean said. "Red, orange, yellow, green, blue, indigo, violet. You've got indigo and violet reversed."

Herman clapped his hands. "Oh, dean, I knew you'd figure it out. Thank you, thank you." He picked up his notebook and ran out of the office.

Once Herman left, the dean tried to concentrate on her writing assignment but the office still seemed full of Herman. Again she wondered why she had taken him on; she seemed to help him more than he helped her. He had been a lab assistant in her previous university. The first time she noticed him was when one of her colleagues found her experiment had been ruined because a stopcock had mysteriously turned to 'on.' As the furious professor ranted, the dean noticed Herman's expression—one of satisfaction. Later, when her colleague had gone, the dean asked Herman if he knew anything about it. He muttered something inaudible. She guessed from the way he shuffled his feet and wouldn't look at her that he was guilty.

After that incident, she took an interest in him. Over time she found out that he came from a large family of thaumaturgists and Sophists. But as a tenth child he was, according to folklore, fey, and thus difficult to bring up. His mother did not have time for him, and he was raised by a sister who eventually took up social work, rather than sophistry, as she said that caring for Herman gave her an interest in people with special needs.

Herman was always fascinated by the heterodoxic arts and wanted to be a thaumaturgist. Although he did well in school, he was refused admission to Weareunder University, to Bogaze, and even to the disreputable college, Buckstar. The dean suspected that he had been rejected because of his appearance. As the same thing had happened to her once, she felt a certain empathy. She started to talk to him about her experiments and to seek his opinion. He was surprisingly well-informed.

Later, when their relationship had developed, she found out that Herman had come upon her colleague manipulating the dials on the dean's equipment. He knew enough to turn them back to their original positions and, in revenge, he had altered the stopcock.

When the dean was informed of her new appointment at UBC, she was also told that she should hire a male on to her otherwise all female faculty. She asked Herman if he would like to accompany her as her personal assistant. Although he lacked the academic qualifications to be a professor, she was able to appoint him as a teaching assistant in the lab. Eventually Henrietta and the students became used to his presence there. In fact, the students found him most helpful, particularly with mathematical calculations. Once accepted, he began to conduct experiments of his own, always telling anyone who inquired that it was the dean's work.

The dean felt guilty about writing papers that described what was essentially Herman's work but, as he had no qualifications, he could not publish. She chided herself for questioning his usefulness when he was largely responsible for her impressive list of publications. And this jamming device might prove to be worth a paper or two for her and a substantial profit for the Academy.

With a sigh, she packed up for the day.

7

Over the next four weeks, Mary Lou was so busy in the library or in the lab that she hardly had time for her friends. She read about ingredients that sounded pleasant, then she tried to obtain them so she could experiment with them. For this, she consulted Professor Meow frequently.

"I have a list of possible ingredients for an imbibing aff," she said on one occasion, "but I don't know where to get them. They're not in our lab."

"What are they? I can probably obtain them," Matilda asked. She was having a good day with her nose so she was prepared to indulge her student.

"The first is Sweet-Scented Spurge Laurel. I like that name."

"Ah, Daphne Indica. It will cause diarrhoea. Good choice," Matilda said.

"Oh no." Mary Lou scratched the name off her list. "The next is Meadow Parsnip. What does that do?"

"What book have you been consulting?" Matilda was impressed by Mary Lou's questions.

"Crawpepper's *Materia Mallefactorum*."[4]

"That's a very advanced text, Mary Lou. Well done. Now, you asked about Meadow Parsnip." Matilda sat up and spoke enthusiastically, as if to a large crowd. "Zizia Aurea is very useful because it is loathsome to the stomach. I believe we have some in our lab if you'd like it?"

"I'll think about it," Mary Lou said. She paused before confessing, "I really want to make a pleasant aff."

Matilda sighed. "What would you like your aff to do? You realise the goal of Sophistry is to increase the irritations humans face? Not to make something pleasant?"

---

4   Eleanor Crawpepper. *Textbook of Materia Mallefactorum*. First published 1654. Reprinted Santas Books, 1964

Mary Lou fiddled with her notes. "Yes, I know. I want my aff to alter taste buds."

"I think you need to decide the function of your aff before you pick ingredients."

"I'm not exactly sure yet. I've been reading about ingredients to get ideas. I like the ones with nice names. Like True Love. Do we have any of that?"

"Paris Quadrifolia. Yes we do. The leaves and berries produce nausea, vomiting and convulsions. Very effective. I'll get you some." Matilda wrote a note to herself.

Mary Lou was awed by the way Matilda immediately said the Latin name for the plants she suggested. The thought reminded her that the study of Sophistry was not a simple matter; would she ever be able to remember all there was to know? And did she want to? She said, "Thank you, but never mind. I'll carry on reading."

Mary Lou left Matilda's office resolved to use only ingredients that she could buy and that she knew had no ill effects. She didn't want to make people sick or have fits, no matter what the goal of Sophistry was. Having made that decision, her work in the lab became easier. She arrived each day with full grocery bags containing condiments, spices, fruits and vegetables that she carefully stacked in her allocated cupboard before preparing her lebes.

Modern sophists had initially experimented with different types of containers for mixing imbibing affirmations and had finally decided that a lebes, a large, flat-bottomed bowl used in ancient Greece, would fit the bill. Original lebes were clay with handles and a stand, but the Royal Guild of Sophists designed bowls of copper, with handles but no stand. They found that copper heated faster than clay and, after an initial hex, would spontaneously kindle when in use.

Although Mary Lou was adept at composing chanting affs that actually energized a brew, she was ignorant of the effects of mixing ingredients. One day, she decided to experiment with fish; not ordinary fish like cod or halibut, but the strangest sea produce she could find. She wandered around a supermarket and put into her basket squid, cod's roes, pickled herring, and anchovies. Satisfied with these basics, she looked for additional ingredients like a vegetable and a carbohydrate. The radishes looked fresh, so she picked up a bunch. In the baking section she found flour and, beside it, a jar of yeast. I wonder what this does, she thought. I'll give it a try.

Back in the lab, Mary Lou stacked her ingredients and washed the radishes. She had a lecture in half an hour, time enough to get her lebes bubbling and throw in the ingredients; first the fish, then the flour, and finally the yeast. She looked at the jar. She didn't know how much she needed and the label gave no help so she threw in the whole jar. Then she left for her lecture.

When she returned to the lab, she could hardly open the door. A giant, grey, doughy mass had taken on an invasive life and was bubbling itself up the walls, out the window, and across the ceiling. Seeing the chance of the open door as a new means to expand, it seeped into the corridor. Mary Lou was too late to close the door; as the dough escaped through this new opening, so too did the malodorous smell of fish. As Mary Lou stood aghast, not knowing what to do, a furious lab assistant appeared out of the dough with splotches of grey goo over his entire body.

"Go and get Professor Meow," he bellowed after he had wiped enough dough off his mouth to speak. Fortunately, Matilda was in her office and came at once. She took one look at the scene, rubbed her talisperson and chanted:

Great mass of fishy, gooey dough,
Into the lebes, back you go.

With obvious reluctance, almost sulkily, the dough oozed backwards, like a movie film in reverse, shrinking itself and settling into Mary Lou's lebes.

"Get rid of it before it can do any more damage," Matilda said. "And," she added, "don't say anything about this mishap to anyone. Do you understand?"

Mary Lou nodded miserably.

The day before her examination, Mary Lou selected her final ingredients. With satisfaction she laid them out on a bench to check she had them all before stacking them in her cleaned lebes. Allspice was one of her choices. She had purchased a pound of it, much to the surprise of the checkout clerk who told her people usually bought an ounce or two. "I need it in the garden," Mary Lou had said. The clerk snickered.

The brown powder was still in its plastic bag. As she picked up the bag it slid from her fingers and spilt its contents on the floor. "Damn," she said to herself. "I should have put it in a jar."

She found a jar in the supplies cupboard and with a small brush swept the spilt powder into it. Gathering up her equipment, she left the lab.

The dean requested that faculty members wear ceremonial regalia for Mary Lou's examination. Although the faculty normally wore their black academic gowns and mortarboards, ceremonial dress consisted of more elaborate black gowns, with coloured chevrons that indicated the alma mater. Gowns for Assistant Professors were made of damask, Associate Professor's gowns were made of silk, and full Professors were elegantly draped in soft velvet gowns, all of them topped with the usual mortar boards.

When the dean arrived in the lecture hall for the examination, Mary Lou was already on the stage with her lebes bubbling so vigorously that steam hung in a damp pall over the stage. Twelve affirmation jars lay on a table ready to receive her brew, the ingredients beside them.

The dean, Matilda, and Ciesta, in her role as Assistant Dean of Student Happenings, joined her on the stage. When the faculty was seated, the dean called for silence. "Thank you for attending Mary Lou's examination. I am sure she will do well. She has been working with Professor Meow and has prepared an imbibing aff that she will now demonstrate." She turned to Mary Lou. "Would you describe your aff to the faculty?"

"It affects the mouths of humans," Mary Lou said.

"Ah, good, we are short of those. Does it render them speechless?" the dean asked.

"Not exactly," Mary Lou answered. "It affects the taste buds."

"Ah, it makes their food taste putrid, is that it?" the dean said.

"Well, no, not really. It's sort of, like…" Mary Lou stammered.

Seeing she was nervous, the dean said, "Proceed."

Matilda cried, "'Tis time, 'tis time," and Mary Lou sprang into action. Dancing around her lebes through the steam, in her purple gown, she resembled a whirling Dervish. As she tossed ingredients into the boiling mass, she rubbed her talisperson and chanted:

In the lebes boil 'til done
Juices of the ripened plum.
Round and round the lebes go
In the nux moschata throw.
Lots of orange carrots got
From a square organic plot.

Single, single, with my jingle;
Mixture blend and juices mingle.

Garlic from the outer clove
Baked 'til brown within the stove.
Purple grapes dried on the vine

Mary Lou's Brew

Vinegar from fermented wine.
A pinch or two of fragrant spice
Makes my concoction super nice.

Single, single, with my jingle;
Mixture blend and juices mingle.

Mary Lou then spooned her concoction into the aff jars and sealed them in the appointed manner. She filled two taster spoons, handed them to Matilda and Ciesta who each took a tentative lick, and disappeared.

8

Mary Lou stood at the front of the lecture hall with her mouth open while the faculty clapped and turned to each other. The dean was surprised. She didn't think that Mary Lou was capable of such a hex. "Well done, Mary Lou," she said. "It's a rare event indeed to see an undergraduate student make a Dissipation aff and then apply it."

"But, but…" Mary Lou stammered. "I didn't mean this to happen"

"Never mind, dear," the dean said. "Now bring them back and all will be well."

"But I don't know how," Mary Lou said, and burst into tears. "I didn't mean this to happen, honestly I didn't. It was meant to be a hex to stimulate the taste buds."

"Did you use a prescribed aff or did you make this up yourself?"

"I made it up myself." Mary Lou groped in her jeans for a tissue. "That's what Matilda told me to do."

There was silence in the lecture hall as the full impact of what had occurred dawned on the faculty. Oh Bloody Spell, the dean thought. Just what I need right now: a student who's managed to dissipate two of my faculty with no counter-aff. Whatever happens, this news *must not* spread around the university.

She turned to face her colleagues. "Does anyone know an antidote for a dissipation aff? What about you, Professor Burghul? This is your field of study, is it not?"

"This could be a case of tetra-metra-pseudo-petra or perhaps, animopomorphosis. Or even, though rare, aerostatic effluviosis," Henrietta said.

"Could you enlighten us as to the differences between them?" The dean asked.

Henrietta, came down to the front, stood behind the podium, placed two arms upon it, leaned forward and cleared her throat.

"Briefly," the dean said.

"Tetra-metra-pseudo-petra is a condition where the subject, or in this case, subjects, are blown to the four winds. Not sky high you understand, but laterally in four directions. The syndrome was first described by Winspooner in 1548 and is to be distinguished from tetra-metra petrifaction. Hence the addition of 'pseudo.'"

Henrietta's voice had turned into a drone and looking around at the drooping faculty, the dean understood why students were always complaining about Henrietta's lectures. Octavia did indeed drop off, and awoke with a start when her head nodded and she nearly fell out of her chair.

"Henrietta, just a brief description of each condition, if you please," the dean interrupted. "There is some urgency here. We wish to reissipate Matilda and Ciesta as speedily as possible. So we know that Tetra-metra-pseudo-petra is scattered to the winds; what about animopo-morphosis?"

Henrietta's voice cackled again as she said sharply, "Animopomorphosis is when the subject is changed into a small creature. Is that all you want to know?"

Henrietta was clearly put out. The dean said, "Only for now. We would like to tap more fully into your expertise later. And the third condition?"

Shaking her head from side to side so that her mortarboard skewed comically over one eye and the tassel brushed her mouth, Henrietta said, "If this is a condition of aerostatic effluviosis, it means they have disappeared into thin air and we will never see them again, as no one has yet discovered the counter-aff. It is an area of great research potential by the way, with many grants available."

"How do we know which condition prevails here?" the dean asked.

"I will need to analyze the aff before I can tell you."

"How long will that take?" The dean spoke sharply. "I am beginning to worry about Matilda and Ciesta."

"This sort of thing is an occupational hazard for academic Sophists as you know. Why, only last year, Priscilla's skin turned tartan after a botched experiment. It was a Black Watch tartan, I recall." Henrietta said.

"Yes, I know. But how long?" The dean said.

"Well, let me see. About 24 hours I think. But I will need Mary Lou's help and unrestricted use of the lab."

"Very well. Mary Lou, you are to work with Professor Burghul to find an antidote to your aff. We will meet back here at the same time tomorrow."

As the faculty prepared to leave, the dean called out, "Just a minute. We must keep quiet about this. We can't have the university thinking our students know how to get rid of faculty. That's all the VP needs to shut us down. And we must put an immediate ban on the collection of creatures, or their parts, by all students. It would be tragic if Matilda and Ciesta have turned into frogs and students pulled out their tongues. I will post a notice but you must notify your students, especially the graduate students. And," she added, "let us all invoke the spirit of the Great Logos that it is not aerostatic effluviosis."

Henrietta left the lecture hall, picked up her bag lunch from her office, and marched across campus to the faculty lab. She thought about how to determine the type of dissipation aff that had so effectively removed Matilda and Ciesta and decided to begin with a literature search. As soon as she entered the lab, she booted up the computer and checked her e-mail. An inquiry about her current research projects from a colleague at McGuiness University distracted her so that she clicked on SPES, the Statistical Package for Enquiring Sophists, and added a few numbers to her data. Then she switched to Wiggle, the search engine, and typed, 'aulophobia' in the search space. "Hmm," she grunted as she viewed the few results, *just* as I thought. No one has done it. Or at least, although they might have tried, no one has succeeded.

Henrietta's research interests included creating fears. She had successfully designed an aff to induce amathophobia, a fear of dust, in a population of British dustmen, and now her attention had turned to aulophobia, a fear of flutes. Once she had created the aff, she intended to test it on the Philadelphia Light Orchestra.

The dustmen experiment had gone so well that the hiring turnover rate had quadrupled. She really should do a follow-up study to determine the average length of time a dustman lasts before quitting. An exploration of the qualities of those who last the longest would be interesting too, but—

A quiet knock at the door interrupted her thoughts. The entire faculty knew the numbers to punch in to open the lock; why don't they just come in? Henrietta thought, annoyed at being disturbed. Maybe they've forgotten. She opened the door and was surprised to see Mary Lou.

"I was supposed to come here after lunch," Mary Lou said.

"Oh, yes. I forgot. Come in." Henrietta guiltily switched off the computer. She should have been thinking about how to reissipate her colleagues instead of contemplating aulophobia, she chided herself. She turned her attention to the problem now at hand.

Mary Lou had never been in the faculty laboratory before, as it was strictly out of bounds to students. Although the benches and equipment were much the same as in the student labs, the jars of powders, bottles of coloured liquids, and baskets of dried animal parts were much more extensive. And the smell was different: it was a strange, exotic smell, the sort that Mary Lou imagined she would find in spice shops in India or the Middle East, and not particularly pleasant.

One bench was completely taken up by a maze of glass tubing that terminated in a beaker of purple, bubbling liquid. Mary Lou walked over to it and followed the maze of purple with her head nodding. Henrietta examined the setup with interest, turned a few screws and adjusted a flow meter. "This is my experiment to see whether I can make traffic lights change to red as soon as a car reaches one," she said. "But now we must concentrate on reissipating Professor Meow and Professor Sands."

"Do you think we'll find out what sort of aff I made?" Mary Lou said. "I mean, soon, today?"

"We're certainly going to try," Henrietta said. Moving over to another, empty, bench she patted it and said to Mary Lou, "Start laying out some equipment while I go and get a lirry."

Mary Lou opened the big drawers under the bench and carefully removed a selection of tubes, corks, beakers, and flasks, although she had no idea what they were going to need. Before long, Henrietta emerged from a side room carrying a small cage that she placed on the bench. It held a creature Mary Lou had never seen, or even imagined, before. It was the size and shape of a rat and had the same ears, but there the resemblance ended. Its body was as green as new spring leaves. When Mary Lou looked closer she could see that, instead of hair, it grew what looked like moss, except on the face, which was smooth and mauve. Enormous cheeks, which seemed as if they were continually blown out, almost hid round, soulful eyes like those of baby seals, except that they were blue. A tiny round mouth blew out air in short puffs, and above that was a square, flat nose with horizontal nostrils. As Mary Lou bent down to peer closer, she sniffed in delight at the odour that emitted from it: it was the smell of chocolate, of such sweetness that Mary Lou wanted to pick up the creature and hug it. But as she reached out, Henrietta said sharply, "No, don't touch. They entice you with their smells and then want to live in your pocket."

"But I don't mind if he lives in my pocket. He's rather beautiful when you get used to him."

"Well, you can't hold it. We are short of them as it is and they are very difficult to metamorphasise. Besides they have rather disturbing, um, turds, which you certainly would not want staining your clothes."

"What are they called?" Mary Lou asked. "I've never seen anything like them before."

"It's a lirrypoop,[5] or lirry for short. A lirrypoop is a silly, empty creature, but they make good experimental animals because of their ability to produce a variety of odours as responses to tests."

"What is this one's name?" Mary Lou bent down to make the same little blowing noises at the creature.

---

5   Oxford English Dictionary. Liripipe, liripoop; a silly person. Obs. 1621 Pilgrim II. Keepe me this young Lirrypoope within doors.

"They don't have names. They are known as WDs—Worker Drudges—and a number." Henrietta looked at the label on the cage. "This one is WD-40."

"Well, I'm going to call it Marvin," Mary Lou said. In response the lirry emitted the smell of roses.

"As you wish. But remember, it's just a silly creature with no brain." Henrietta recoiled as the lirry blew a raspberry along with a choking, sulphurous gas. Holding a handkerchief to her nose, Henrietta said to it, "I'm sorry, I didn't mean that. What would the world be without lirrypoops? Our science couldn't proceed without them."

"What are we going to do with him?" Mary Lou asked.

"We're going to watch its reaction to your aff," Henrietta said, still wiping her eyes, "as a first step in the analysis." The gas dissipated and Henrietta's eyes stopped watering. "Now we must get on. Where are your ingredients?"

"They're still in the lecture hall. Shall I go and get them?"

"We shall need the jars, your lebes, and all the ingredients. I will come and help you. Bring this cart to put everything on."

They entered through the back door of the lecture hall that led straight on to the stage. Mary Lou's lebes was still there, as were the ingredients and jars. They loaded everything on to the cart, then Mary Lou said, "That's funny. There's only eleven jars here. One is missing."

"It can't be," Henrietta said. "Count again."

"No, there are only eleven—see."

"Are you absolutely sure there were twelve to begin with?"

"Absolutely. And Professor Meow checked them too."

They stared at one another in growing horror. "That means someone has taken one," Henrietta said. "And I wonder what black mischief they will get up to."

9

As the faculty filed out after Mary Lou's disastrous examination, Prunella pretended to be busy with some papers. She did not want her colleagues to see her delight over Matilda and Ciesta's disappearance and instead of asking the Great Logos that it not be aerostatic effluviosis, she rubbed her talisperson and wished that it were. Now all she had to do was obtain some of Mary Lou's brew, and the answer to her disposal problem would be in her hands.

As soon as everyone left the lecture hall, Prunella strolled casually down to the front. She made out that she was simply examining the ingredients but, taking a quick look around, she grabbed a jar of brew, slipped it into the pocket of her gown, and quickly left through the back door.

In her office, Prunella hid the jar behind her *Encyclopaedia Mysteriatica* and then sat staring at the wall wondering how to proceed. The list of names lay on her desk: Matilda, Ciesta, Octavia, Wanda. She crossed out Matilda and Ciesta. Two down, two to go. Mary Lou's brew was an Alphasend. All she had to do was get the senior faculty to take it. But how? And who to start with? Octavia or Wanda? She would start with Octavia; Wanda was far too powerful. Then there would be the dean to deal with, but that could wait. If she didn't get tenure, she would only have to go to the administration with the story of the disappearing faculty and—she cackled at the thought—that would be the end of the school.

Octavia chaired the Curriculum Committee on which Prunella sat. There would be a meeting tomorrow. Coffee was normally served during meetings and Prunella thought about how she could slip some of Mary Lou's brew into Octavia's coffee. But no, that would not do. If Octavia vanished in front of the others they would guess what had happened and would suspect Prunella. She had to find Octavia alone, but how?

"Go to her office, of course," she said out loud. There were several committee matters she could discuss. She would go on the pretext of suggesting a design for the new course, Sorcery and its Antecedents, which the committee was dealing with. But once there, how could she get the brew into Octavia? Grab her and force it down her throat? No, that would be too uncouth. She was, after all, an academic, and needed subtler means of pulling down a rival.

Suddenly Prunella remembered a song from *The Sound of Music*: "Just a spoonful of sugar makes the medicine go down, the medicine go down…" Yes, she would conceal the potion in some form of candy. Fudge would be best, as it is pliable. She could conceal the brew inside a piece then mould it back into shape.

She found her propellant, took off her robe, put on her outdoor cloak, locked her office, and prepared to transmit to Grabville Market from the faculty launching pad. On the way, she sang to herself:

Just a spoonful of potion makes Octavia go poof,
Octavia go poof, Octavia go poof,
Just a spoonful of potion makes Octavia go poof,
In the most dramatic way.

After telling Herman that she was not to be disturbed, the dean entered her office and put a hex on the door so that it could not be opened. She had not had time to reflect on the events of the morning and she wished to consider possible courses of action.

From a concealed cupboard she pulled out a hand-blown glass hookah and a small packet of BC Best Bud. She filled the hookah with water, crushed a pinch of bud into the bowl, lit it by applying a hex and took a satisfied pull on the mouthpiece. She wanted to inhale just enough to clear her mind but not so much that she experienced a high.

A La-z Boy chair, with a small table beside it to hold the hookah, was strategically placed so the dean could stare out of the window. Stretched out smoking pot was the dean's coping mechanism, one where she entertained her most creative ideas and dealt with her most disturbing emotions. Gazing out of the window, however, was no longer as peaceful as it had been when all she could see was trees and the sky. Now she had to look at the newly constructed Centre for Post-Graduate Studies. Mercifully, it was near completion, so she no longer had to put up with the noise, but she was forever doomed to stare at the pink concrete block kindly endowed by the widow of the late Lord Otterbrook.

Post-graduate studies indeed! Sophistry was one of the oldest professions, and yet her school was housed in decrepit buildings scattered across campus. Not only that, the lecture halls for general use had to be booked and Wanda, who was in charge of scheduling, reported at the start of term that the only times available for Sophistry were at 6 a.m. or 5 p.m. Fortunately, Wanda was no wuss and had scared the wits out of the booking clerk who quickly saw the error of his ways.

But to the business at hand: what more could she do to recover Matilda and Ciesta? She knew very well that no matter what Henrietta discovered, someone, probably Octavia, would want to strike a committee to look into the affair. There would be an argument about who would chair it and who would sit on it; they would request secretarial time and extra paper for their report; meetings would drag on until no one could remember who Matilda and Ciesta were. No. Action had to be taken at once.

Above all, the dean did not want the Vice President to find out she had lost two faculty members, especially if they were not recovered. Other schools of Sophistry around the world accepted these sorts of events as occupational hazards and thought them regrettable, but inevitable. Fortunately, teachers from other disciplines on campus were unlikely to find out about the disappearance of the two faculty as they were in awe of, even frightened of, Sophists, so they did not interact much. And anyway, the dean knew too much about the doings of some important professors for them to point fingers at her. It was the senate and governors that were the trouble.

She inhaled long and deep, gazed at the pink, concrete monstrosity outside her window, and pondered. What had happened to the architects of the day? They seemed to have no sense of beauty or balance, and to have lost touch with the idea of the importance of architecture on the human spirit.

She often wondered why she was different. She did not subscribe to the notion that busyness equalled productivity, as so many of her faculty clearly did. Some people seemed to believe that if their calendars were filled with meeting engagements, they were usefully employed. The dean preferred to measure results.

As a junior professor, her liberal views had got her into trouble. Now she was the dean, with some power and control, she kept meetings to a minimum, much to the consternation of the older faculty. One of her first actions on receiving the appointment was to abolish at least eleven rules, rules that had been instituted in most cases by the Great Griselda, a former, autocratic dean. The current dean had taken a great deal of pleasure in revoking such dictates as only quills are to be used for writing; faculty members are to sign in and out on a chalkboard in their building entrance; mortarboard tassels are to fall to the front. After a few weeks, she had been able to point out that the school had not collapsed without these restrictive rules; indeed, it had flourished.

She closed her eyes and inhaled deeply. Her mind drifted to her appointment as dean. If she hadn't had the support of a renowned thaumaturgist, Dr. Circando Kuroko, she might never have risen in the professorial ranks. But as her supervisor and mentor in the co-educational college she had attended, he promoted her as intelligent, innovative, and forward-thinking. She didn't like to tell him that these same qualities prompted many people to dislike her and try to impede her progress.

She thought of Circando with affection. It was his sense of humour that she enjoyed the most—not an abundant quality in thaumaturgists, or Sophists, for that matter. Her friends often remarked that she seemed amused when she was attempting to be serious and dignified. But what could be funnier than people's behaviour?

Feeling better, she took one last draw on her hookah, put it away, and prepared to tackle the day's problems.

10

Henrietta wheeled Mary Lou's equipment into the lab and they unloaded it on to a bench. "Lay out your ingredients in the order in which you used them," she ordered Mary Lou. "First, we shall just have the lirry sniff each one and note its reaction. I want you to keep records. Here's a clipboard. Draw three columns. Label the first, 'Ingredient,' the second, 'lirry's reaction,' and the third, 'time.' "

"Why time?" Mary Lou asked.

"We need to know how long it took the lirry to react. Or even if it reacted at all."

"Why?"

"I don't really know," Henrietta said. "But we have to start somewhere. Now what was your first ingredient?"

"Plum juice." Mary Lou held up a large jar.

"Pour a few drops into this beaker. Be careful to make it a few drops as we may need more later. Now hold it in front of the lirry while I set a stop watch."

Mary Lou waved the beaker in front of the cage. "Here Marvin, what do you think of that?" The lirry made little sucking noises with its tiny mouth and after a few moments Mary Lou could smell something she could not identify.

"Forty-five seconds," Henrietta said. "Write that down. And the smell is, let me see—" She bent down, closed her eyes and sniffed several times. "Custard," she pronounced. "Bird's. Now try the next ingredient, which is what?"

"Nux moschata. Nutmeg," Mary Lou said. She took a pinch of the powder and waved her fingers under the lirry's nose. After a while the lirry produced an odour and Mary Lou noted the information on the chart.

"Carry on, Mary Lou. Show me the chart when you've finished." Henrietta moved to her study on traffic lights and started to draw up purple fluid with a pipette. The experiment was at a critical stage and she wanted to attend to it even though she knew that the analysis of Mary Lou's brew took priority. But weeks of work lay in the purple liquid, and she had no intention of wasting it. She glanced at the clock. Time management, she thought. I will allow myself 30 minutes on each task. Mary Lou was doing the first necessary tests, so she would attend to her own work until the student had finished.

When Mary Lou had tested all the ingredients her chart looked like this:

Ingredient	Lirry's Reaction	Time
Plum juice	Custard	45 secs
Nutmeg	Baked apple	41 secs
Carrots	Donkey	63 secs
Garlic	Sausage	5 secs
Raisins	Toast	25 secs
Vinegar	French fries	90 secs
Spice	Sneezed	

She showed it to Henrietta. "What's this?" Henrietta said, pointing to the word 'sneezed.'

"He didn't make a smell. He just sneezed until I took the powder away."

"Here, let me try." Henrietta held out a pinch of spice. The lirry's nose twitched several times and then it made an 'achhoo' noise.

"You're right. I've never seen a lirry sneeze before. What sort of spice is it?" Henrietta asked.

"The container said allspice but I don't really know what was in it. Do you think that's the cause of the trouble?" Mary Lou looked anxious. She didn't want to tell Henrietta that she had dropped the spice on the floor before using it in her aff. Logos knows what she had swept up with the spice—could be anything. She decided to keep quiet about the accident; they were analysing her aff anyway, and the mystery ingredient might be revealed.

"Never, never make an aff without knowing exactly what you're putting in it." Henrietta sounded cross. "Didn't Matilda tell you that?"

"Well, yes," Mary Lou said. "But I thought allspice was Jamaica pepper. It comes from a tree that grows there—the *Pimento dioica* plant. Professor Inn told us about it in one of her lectures."

"It can be," said Henrietta, "but it can also be Carolina allspice or Japan allspice or wild allspice. If it is wild, then it may contain any number of constituents depending on where it grew. For example, wild allspice from Scotland may have haggis in it and some from Saskatchewan must have frozen before it was ground." She sighed and sat on a stool. "Where shall we go from here?" she asked, more to herself than to Mary Lou.

"We could ask Marvin to react to the whole potion," Mary Lou said.

"Yes, I thought of that but I don't want it to disappear too."

"Well I sniffed it when I was experimenting and I didn't disappear," Mary Lou said. But of course she was using spice before she dropped it. What was she going to do if they couldn't find them? She wouldn't be able to stay in the Academy. Not that she particularly wanted to, but even if she did want to, she couldn't. She would be known as the student who dissipated two teachers for the rest of her life. And she'd never get into another program or even into another college. Who would take someone who made people vanish? She wouldn't be able to get a job either; not even at McDonald's. They'd assume that when she said, "Do you want fries with that?" there would be a poof, and away would go the customer, burger and all.

"Well if you didn't disappear, let's try it," Henrietta said. "We can always use another lirry if this one vanishes."

Mary Lou spooned some of her aff into a beaker and held it against Marvin's cage. Then she had to step back quickly as a strong, sweet smell enveloped her.

"Skunk!" Henrietta said as she rapidly moved to the other side of the lab. "I wonder what that means. Do you suppose the professors have turned into skunks? And if they have, how do we get them back?"

11

Matilda sniffed. A dank smell of leaf mould assailed her nostrils but she could not discover the source as she was in almost total darkness. She tried to walk but, to her surprise, she was on her hands and knees. Where on earth was she? A minute ago she was on the stage of a lecture hall watching Mary Lou perform her chanting aff. She had been given a taste of brew; she remembered that, but then what? Had she gone blind? She couldn't hear anything either. Had she gone deaf as well?

Just then there came a thud as though someone had banged his head and a voice said, "A thousand horrid hexes!"

"Who's that?" Matilda said.

"Ciesta. I'm stuck between something. Is that you, Matilda?"

"Yes. Where are we? I can't see a thing."

"Neither can I. Are we in the basement? How did we get here?"

"I haven't any idea. Look, there's a chink of light over there. Let's head for it."

"Where? Oh yes. I can't move very well," Ciesta said. "I seem to be on all fours. And my body is jammed."

"I'm on my hands and knees also. I think we may be underground judging by the smell. And you know that I have a very refined sense of smell." Matilda reached the chink of light shining through vertical wooden boards and peered through. "I can see a garden, I think. There's a bush, then a lawn, then I can't see beyond that."

The noise of an automobile grew in volume and came to rest above their heads. The engine stopped. Two car doors slammed. A female voice said, "David dear, I think we've got a skunk under the garage again."

"Yes, I can smell it too. Call the exterminator, Doris dear. He'll come and set traps for it."

"Why don't we just put poison down, David dear."

"I keep telling you, Doris dear, that we can't do that. We'd end up with rotting skunk bodies where we can't reach them, and the smell would be something else again. No, let the authorities come and deal with it."

Footsteps receded and there was silence. Matilda said, "We must get out of here and ask David dear and Doris dear where we are." She pushed at a loose board with her head until finally it swung to one side. She looked around for Ciesta and in the dim light saw an extremely fat skunk wedged between the wall and a bucket. "Ciesta, is that you?"

"Matilda? That can't be you. All I can see … is a skunk … with a long nose." Ciesta giggled. "You look most odd."

"You are a skunk too," Matilda said. "Do you realize what that stupid girl has done? She's changed us into skunks! And now we're going to be trapped. And after all the help I gave her too. I spent hours tutoring her."

"Yes, well she was certainly… successful with her aff. You are to be congratulated… for tutoring her so well," Ciesta said in her usual breathless manner. She struggled to pull herself out. "Come and give my rear end… a push, will you?"

Matilda stood behind Ciesta, put her snout against her tail and pushed. Nothing happened. She pushed again.

"Harder," Ciesta said. "I'm nearly out."

Matilda backed up and readied herself for a run at the rear end of the fat skunk. "One, two, three," she shouted and charged. Ciesta shot out and fell on her nose. She lay breathing heavily for a moment and then started to laugh.

"I see nothing funny in this situation. We are trapped under a garage, we don't know where we are, and we may be left like this forever." Matilda sounded as if she was crying but there were no tears in her beady, black eyes. "If we ever return to normal and I get my hands on Mary Lou, I'll, I'll… I should *never* have taken her on. Why didn't we just send her off to pursue another career? As a vet, or a zoologist or something, seeing she likes animals so much." Matilda's snout began to twitch furiously. "Well, it's too late now. We must deal with this situation as best we can and keep our heads. Although we have the form of skunks, we can still think and talk to each other. So let us keep calm and consider our options." Matilda lay down. She tried to sit but found out that skunks only have two positions, up or down. "First we must get out of here."

"I think we should stay right here," Ciesta said. "It's warm and dry."

"How do you think anyone will find us here?" Matilda's irritation came through in her voice.

"How will anyone find us anywhere?"

"Exactly," Matilda said in the tone of one addressing a particularly stupid student. "That is why we need to get back to college. Then someone will find us and give us the counter-aff."

"Does anyone know what that is?" Ciesta asked.

"We are obviously under an animopo-morphic dissipation hex. I do have the counter-aff somewhere. I can't remember where. It must be in my files in my office. But I remember it's one that has to be imbibed. A chant, I could intone and we would reissipate."

"What if no-one else…knows the counter-aff?" Ciesta said. "How can you tell them…that you have the recipe?"

"We must calm down, Ciesta and think," Matilda said.

"I am quite calm," Ciesta said. "It's you that's nervous."

"I am in perfect control of myself," Matilda said. There was silence for a while before she continued. "When we get back to the college, I will show the file to someone. But first, we need to be found by someone who realizes who we are."

"How do we know if people…can hear us? We can hear each other… but our speech may be…indecipherable to humans."

They heard footsteps approaching and quickly concealed themselves behind a pile of old crates. More light came in as someone removed a few vertical boards. A female voice said, "I thought we had this boarded up pretty well so I don't know how you got in. There, this will let you out, skunk. Now go. Go and find yourself somewhere else to live and don't come back."

Matilda called out, "Doris dear, can you hear me?" There was no reply. She shouted, "Hello, hello, Doris dear. Ciesta, shout with me. Hello there, hello there." They heard footsteps recede.

"Oh dear," Matilda said. "Obviously we cannot speak to humans."

Ciesta groaned. "I've just remembered…the third year students are to collect smell…of skunk for next week's phylactery class. That means we could lose…our anal glands. Can skunks live without their anal glands?"

"You never worried about that before," Matilda said. "Oh dear, apart from the students, all sorts of dangers await us: dogs, cars, coyotes, the exterminator. We'll be lucky if we make it back to the college even if we do find out where we are. What time is it?"

"I don't know. I don't have a watch on. I did, but I don't now. I wonder where it went?" Ciesta said.

"Never mind, let's just wait until dusk and then we'll leave."

"I think we should leave now. While we can see…where we are going."

"I think we should wait until it's dark. Skunks are nocturnal so we should be able to see in the dark."

"I still think we should leave now. There are many dangers in the dark."

"There are many dangers in the light too. We have a better chance of concealing ourselves in the dark. Under hedges, for example." Matilda curled up as if to go to sleep. "You leave on your own if you want. I'm waiting until dark."

Ciesta sighed and said, "Okay, have it your way." She was silent for a while and then, "What colour is my stripe?"

"Red."

"Same as when I was a human," Ciesta said. "Does it suit me?"

Matilda snorted. "How should I know?" She wanted to say that red tints hadn't suited Ciesta as a human so why should it be attractive in a skunk, but she refrained. Ciesta had always got on her nerves; there was something irreverent about her manner that Matilda, a stickler for protocol, found disturbing.

Ciesta sat on the Standing Committee for Seats and Stools, which Matilda chaired. The purpose of the committee was to assess, repair, and obtain seating in the school and dormitories. One day, when they were evaluating the utility of a Morris chair with an intricately woven seat, Ciesta had bounced on it so hard that the webbing broke and left her firmly wedged in the wooden frame. Matilda had had to send for a carpenter to extract her. While the committee was concerned about the loss of the chair and the expense of the whole episode, Ciesta had laughed heartily and said, "I hope my errant rear…hasn't put us in arrears."

Matilda sighed. Oh, good Logos, she thought, why did I have to end up in this predicament with Ciesta?

"What does it feel like…to you…to be a skunk?" Ciesta asked.

"Same as you, I suppose," Matilda said. "I don't like it. Everything looks very big. I'm getting a crick in my neck from looking up."

"I feel itchy." Ciesta scratched her head with a paw. "I think I've got fleas."

"You probably have. Skunks do. Get used to it." Matilda was in no mood for small talk.

"I'm hungry. What do skunks eat?"

"How should I know?" Matilda curled herself into a ball. "I'm tired. I'm going to sleep."

"What did you have for breakfast?" Ciesta asked. Matilda did not answer. "I had pancakes. But that was hours ago. I wonder if skunks like pancakes. Matilda, how would you fancy…a pancake? With maple syrup?"

Matilda rolled over. "We have been turned into skunks. We may be run over, exterminated by a pest control officer, chased by dogs, never reissipated, and all you can talk about is pancakes. Good grief, give me a break."

"That's what I was talking about," Ciesta said. "Give me a break…fast."

Matilda groaned and turned her back on Ciesta.

12

The dean tried to concentrate on the paper she was to present at MAST (Meeting of Academic Sophists and Thaumaturgists) to be held in a few days. Supposed to present, she thought ruefully. She wondered if she could still go now that two of her faculty had disappeared. Perhaps not for the whole three days, but if she transmitted overnight, presented her paper and transmitted back, she would only be away one day. But that would not give her time to do the networking she needed to do in order to secure a place on the Great Sophist Council and that, not her paper, was the main reason for her attendance.

A quick knock on the door and Herman bounded in. "Success at last," he said. "I have finally worked out all the electrical readings. The jammer will work. Now it needs you to hex it and I can start preliminary trials."

"Great news, Herman. Congratulations."

"When can you come to the lab?"

"Not right now. You heard about Mary Lou's brew? Well, she and Henrietta are in the lab working on finding out the nature of the dissipation aff. So we can't work on the jammer until they've finished, I'm afraid."

Herman looked disappointed. "Yes, I heard. When will they be finished?"

"I don't know." The dean leaned back in her chair and yawned. "I'm trying to finish the paper I'm supposed to present at MAST. I was hoping to attend but I suppose I can't while two of my faculty have vanished. What do you think?"

Herman began to sway. "Not until you know what the hex is that Matilda and Ciesta are under. It would look as if you don't care."

"Yes, you're right."

But whether she presented the paper or not, she was still submitting it to the *Journal of Applied Hermetic Research,* and it needed editing. She picked up her red pen and settled herself to the task.

Jennifer Craig

The Effect of Two Types of Plastic CD Packaging on Wrap-rage

Introduction

Hard-to-remove packaging is leading to a satisfying increase in what the British term "wrap-rage." A survey conducted by the University of Melton Mowbray[6] found that 99% of respondents thought that packaging had got harder to open in the past 10 years and 71% reported they had been injured as they struggled to open packaging. However, there is still one product where people, particularly young people, are not challenged enough: compact disks, although wrapped in plastic, remain too easy to open. The purpose of this study was to increase the level of wrap-rage in compact disk buyers by encasing the plastic box in an impenetrable material (IM).

Method

Procedure.

Two types of impenetrable material (IM) were designed using ordinary plastic wrap (PW) as the base. In each case 100 sheets of PW $36cm^2$ were used.

IM1. 100 sheets of PW were subjected to electrofrenetic blasts of 5 minutes with a 10-minute recovery time for a total of 60 minutes of blast. (12 x 5 times.)

IM2. 100 sheets of PW were soaked in a solution of Thermatite for 72 hours and then hung to dry in a wind chamber for 24 hours.

IM3. 100 sheets of ordinary plastic wrap.

300 compact disks (CDs) of the popular singer, Ringin Abelli, were wrapped in one of the three types of wrap using a standard Ripoff machine with the same settings for each type. (12 r.p.m. x 5,600 t.t.f.)

---

6   Pie, P. "A telephone survey to determine estimates of difficulty in extracting objects from packages." *Journal of Activities of Daily Living*, (209) 5-8, 2001

Subjects.

Subjects were high school and undergraduate university students who were shopping for CDs of Ringin Abelli. They were offered a 10% discount if they agreed to 1) unwrap the CD in the store and then 2) complete a Frustration Index. (FI).

The Frustration Index was a simple Likert scale where subjects indicated their level of frustration on a scale of 1 – No Frustration to 10 – Over the Top.

Results.

Results are reported for 299 subjects. (One young man attacked his CD with a compass from his geometry set that stuck in his palm and had to be surgically removed.)

Package	#Subjects	FI
IM1	100	8.5
IM2	99	9.3
IM3	100	1.2

Analysis of Variance showed no statistical difference between IM1 and IM2, $p \geq 0.5$. IM3 was so different that no statistical analysis was required.

Discussion

The frustration level when unwrapping a CD covered in ordinary plastic was negligible, thus lending support to the underlying hypothesis that present packaging is inadequate. Both types of experimental wrap produced high levels of wrap-rage. As there was no statistical difference between the reported frustration levels, either could be used to effect. However, the wrap soaked in Thermatite and hung to dry was easier to prepare than the wrap subjected to electro-frenetic blasts. For this reason, the recommendation is that CD manufacturers use Thermatite.

As the dean was considering how to re-word the last sentence, a loud knock on the door was followed by the uninvited entry of Thea Terlecki, a graduate student, accompanied by six others. "What's this ban on collecting animal parts?" Thea demanded without ceremony.

"Do come in," the dean said. She leaned back and regarded Thea calmly. "Two of my faculty members were accidentally dissipated. We think they may be small animals. Until we find them, a ban is necessary."

"Who dissipated them?" Thea said.

"It doesn't really matter, does it?" the dean said.

"Was it one of us?" another student asked.

"It was a student, yes." The dean narrowed her eyes. Thea did not seem to pick up this warning signal.

"A graduate student?"

"No. An undergraduate student. She made a mistake, as we all do from time to time. It was not intentional; however, the consequences must be dealt with rationally."

The dean regretted that the ethical code governing faculty included a prohibition on putting hexes on students. She would have liked to use her talisperson and cause a zipper to be placed across Thea's mouth. The hex had once worked well on a belligerent lawyer who had unwisely threatened the dean during a Chancellor's meeting. She still took pleasure in the memory of him trying to unzip his mouth in order to speak.

"Which undergraduate student?" Thea's face was red with fury.

The dean sucked her teeth. If she didn't give the name they would find out anyway and then there would be more trouble. "Mary Lou, in second year," she said after some hesitation. "And," she added, "we will never reissipate the faculty if anything happens to her." She stared pointedly at Thea and then at the other students. "I will be keeping a close eye on Mary Lou. Any attempt at retaliation will be met by severe consequences."

Thea's expression changed from anger to distress. "Do you realise I need spider legs urgently if I am to complete my experiment to turn political windbags into Highland bagpipes? It was your suggestion, you know; and you are my supervisor." Thea was nearly in tears. "And my comps are next week."

"So are mine," another student said. "And I need gall of goat tomorrow so I can get my paper done in time."

All the students talked at once, each saying how they were being held up by the ban. The dean raised her hand. "Calm down," she said. "I don't think it will take long before we find the faculty. And then the ban will be lifted. In the meantime I will grant you unlimited extensions …" She realised that a couple of the students would take years if she allowed them unlimited time. "No—on second thought, extensions for twice as long as the ban is in effect. If anyone has difficulty with time, then please see me individually."

"My experiment will be ruined," Thea said. "I will have to start all over again."

"Thea, what exactly do you need?" the dean said. She got up. "Come with me to our lab and I will see if I can provide you with your requirements. Is there anyone else in the same boat? No. Good. Very well, Thea, let's go."

13

Prunella returned from Grabville Market and gleefully laid a box of fudge on her desk. She tried a piece. Mmm, she loved fudge. She tried another, chocolate this time. Then vanilla with nuts. She sucked her fingers and closed her eyes to fully savour the texture and taste of each delectable square. Another piece then she'd get on with doctoring some. My, this was good. Just one more and she'd stop. Licking her lips, she opened her eyes to see with astonishment that she had eaten it all. I can't believe I ate the whole lot, she thought. Now I have to go back for more.

By the time she returned again, the afternoon was well advanced. "I better hurry, or I'll be too late to catch Octavia," she said to herself. She took an Exacto knife out of her drawer, sliced three pieces of fudge in half crosswise and made small holes in the bottom halves. She found a dropper and opened the jar of aff. The contents had solidified into a jam-like consistency so instead of the dropper, she used a nail file to spread a little on each fudge half.

"I wonder how much you need?" she muttered. "Matilda and Ciesta only took the merest sip, so this should be enough. Anyway, if it doesn't work on Octavia, I can always try Wanda."

She carefully placed the halves of fudge together and massaged them smooth. Now, how was she to distinguish the fixed fudge from the rest so that she wouldn't eat the wrong ones? She had to sit and think for a while before deciding to empty the good fudge on to a saucer, leaving only the doctored ones in the box. I'll offer the box to Octavia and say that I've eaten too much already, she decided.

Prunella gathered up her course plans and the box of fudge. She looked around before leaving. "Better hide the aff jar in case someone comes in," she said as she put everything down again in order to pull out the *Encyclopaedia Mysteriatica* and conceal the jar. She walked across campus to Octavia's office. As Octavia was a full Professor, she had an office with a window, in contrast to Prunella, who worked in an airless room not much bigger than a closet.

"Ingress," a wavery voice said after Prunella knocked.

"Octavia, do you have time to look at my ideas for the new course?" Prunella said as she entered the room. "I wanted to run them by you before the meeting tomorrow."

"Yes, come in and sit down. Would you like a cup of tea?" Octavia got up to plug in an electric kettle as Prunella sat down beside her desk.

"I'm glad you came, as I value your educational expertise on our committee," Octavia said in her weak little voice. She moved back to her chair. Her thin body on stick-like legs did not seem strong enough to support what lay beneath her billowy gown, so that she looked as if she was in permanent danger of toppling over. She nearly fell sideways as she lowered herself into her chair.

Prunella stared in astonishment. She was unused to praise. She began to feel guilty about her plot to dispose of Octavia; perhaps Octavia would support her application for tenure and she had chosen the wrong one. But Octavia could be influenced by the others, who would persuade her to vote with them. She gave herself a shake, and said, "Thank you, it's nice to be appreciated. Here are tentative objectives I wrote for the course. I am sure they are not complete or even what you want, but they can form the basis for discussion. We have to start somewhere."

She laid a piece of paper before Octavia on which was written:

Sorcery and its Antecedents Course Objectives.

1. Evaluate the effectiveness of the use of lapis lazuli talispersons in medieval England.
2. Trace the historical significance of the use of lebes and other containers in the practice of Sophistry.
3. Discuss the ethical dilemmas presented by the use of Dissipation affs.
4. Analyze three historical research articles that demonstrate the higher energy in the tails of animals.

Octavia started to read the list. When the kettle boiled she got up to make tea in an earthenware pot that wore a pink-and-white knitted cozy. She handed a pink cup and saucer to Prunella before sitting down again. "Help yourself to sugar and milk," she said.

"Thank you." Prunella looked around to observe a row of binders covered in pink Mactac, a picture of pink flowers, and a surrealist print in pink and black. "You seem to be very fond of pink."

"Yes, I am," Octavia said. She paused. "I am the youngest of eight and I have seven older brothers. Everyone kept forgetting I was a girl, which was okay until they enrolled me in Steam Train Racing. I didn't want to play that stupid game—all those boys chasing steam trains around a field and falling over tracks that climbed up man-made hills and crossed over man-made rivers. I could think of more intelligent pastimes." Octavia stirred her tea and took a sip. "So I decided to wear pink to remind everyone that I am female. I decorated my room pink, too. Then I got into the habit and it never left me, I'm afraid. Anyhow, enough of that. Let me look at the objectives again."

She picked up the sheet of paper, stroked a cluster of pink hairs that jutted from her wizened chin, and read. "Well done, Prunella. These will give the committee something to work on. Let us take each one and go over it. I see you have restricted talispersons to those made only of lapis lazuli. What about copper or even those made from cows' tails?"

Prunella stopped gazing at Octavia's gown, a worn, possibly antique garment with, was that egg down the front? "We really want the students to evaluate talispersons and rather than confuse them with too many types, I thought it best if they concentrated on one so that they could spend their time in critical analysis. But it doesn't have to be lapis lazuli, it could be copper."

"Yes, I see," Octavia said. She gazed out of the window. "My first talisperson was made with a cow's tail. A Hertfordshire cow—no, that's not right. Was it Hampshire? Hereford, Hertfordshire or Hampshire—one of those. Anyway, it was pure black with one white hair. Not very powerful. I had to replace it when..."

"Oh, by the way, would you like a piece of fudge?" Prunella proffered the box to interrupt the flow of talk. "I was in Grabville Market today and I have a weakness for fudge." She laughed. "I rather over-did it, so you would be doing me a favour by eating some." Octavia took a piece of fudge and laid it on the blotter on her desk. "Thank you.

Now the second objective—I like that. I think it's important that students know about the origin of their rituals and don't just do them because we say so." She leaned back. "I remember when I was a young gal, an undergraduate student. I thought the ritual of Flipping the Fylfot[7] was ridiculous, and it wasn't until I went to the library and read about Hortense the Horrible that I changed my mind."

---

7 Fylfot: identical to a swastika. The ceremony of Flipping the Fylfot involved pinning a metal fylfot to a post and beating it with a caduceus so that it spun. Thought to induce scrofula. Michaela B. *Sophist Rituals and Practices*, 1934.

Prunella felt like screaming, "Eat the fudge," but instead she said, as calmly as she could, "Yes, anything to encourage them to do library research."

Pink fingernails reached for the fudge. Prunella held her breath, but Octavia put the candy back on the blotter and picked up the paper again. "An ethical question. Good. I think it is so important to instil a sense of ethical responsibility into the students, don't you? Especially about Dissipation affs, which can so easily go wrong."

She picked up the fudge and this time, popped it into her mouth. Within one nanosecond, she had vanished.

Prunella jumped to her feet and danced around the office, whooping. Then she sang her "Spoonful of Potion" ditty again. She sat at Octavia's desk and imagined herself in a similar office. A group of third year students passed by on their propellants. She ducked under the desk until they were out of sight. If there was an investigation into Octavia's disappearance she didn't want students to report that she had been in her office.

Octavia's mortarboard with its gold tassel denoting a full Professor lay on the desk. Prunella stroked the black velvet before placing it on her head. As an Associate Professor, hers would only have a silver tassel but that would be better than an amber one. She saw herself holding seminars with graduate students who would look at her with respect and admiration as she discussed her research with them. They would make up for the inevitable frustration of working with the dodos and besides, with her new rank, she would be able to avoid them and go her own way.

In her reverie, without thinking, she popped a piece of fudge into her mouth.

14

Mary Lou yawned and looked at her watch. For the last two hours she had been presenting Marvin with two ingredients at a time, and all that happened was he gave out two smells. For example, when shown nutmeg and plum juice, he emitted the smells of baked apple and custard. Eventually he grew tired, turned his back on Mary Lou, put his head between his front legs, and snored gently.

Mary Lou wandered across the lab to where Henrietta was peering down a microscope. "How are you getting on?" Mary Lou inquired.

Henrietta had decided that the active ingredient in the aff lay in the allspice and she was trying to isolate it. A row of beakers and a crate of test tubes containing different coloured fluids, each carefully labelled, gave testimony to her work.

"I've eliminated a number of possibilities," she said, leaning back to stretch, "but this test may help." She pointed to three petri dishes. "I have mixed the spice with three types of separating gel but they take a few minutes to work. Did you find any changes in the lirry?"

"No. He's gone to sleep. And I'm hungry," Mary Lou said. "When are we going to stop?"

"We're not. We may be up all night. But I'll send for a pizza. You put the kettle on and make tea. Everything's in that little kitchen." Henrietta indicated a door near the entrance that Mary Lou had not noticed before. Henrietta moved to the phone, dialled, and returned to the microscope.

When the pizza arrived, they sat in the kitchen to eat. "Why don't we try another lirry?" Mary Lou asked with her mouth full.

"No need. Correlation studies were done decades ago and they have a very high inter-rater reliability index."

"I meant, so I can carry on," Mary Lou said.

"Oh. Yes. Well, I don't think there's much point in trying more combinations. I'm pretty certain the answer lies in the allspice." Henrietta removed an olive that had stuck on one of her long nails and rubbed tomato sauce off her gown with her knuckles, causing yet another stain. "You can help me with the separating tests. The gel should be ready now."

When they had finished eating, Mary Lou put the remains of the pizza in the kitchen fridge, washed up, and returned to the lab.

"Now scrape a small portion of the jelly from the first petri dish on to each of these dishes until you have twelve, and I'll do the same with the second petri dish. Here, let me show you." Henrietta took a pile of glass dishes, like tiny saucers, and laid them out in three rows of four. Then, with a wooden spatula, she scraped gel from the first petri dish and put a blob on a saucer. "You do the same with them all."

Eventually they had 36 saucers of gel laid out in three sets, one set of twelve for each petri dish. "Now, I am going to test each one with a different acid. I'll start with seweratic acid." Henrietta carefully squirted one drop of acid on to the first of each set of twelve saucers.

"What are we looking for?" Mary Lou asked.

"The petri dishes contain gamma-mamma-osmium chloride, tellalytou-ethyl and strontium hexa-silicatum. I am hoping to see a reaction with one of twelve acids. There is none with this acid, so we'll try furioustic acid next." She spilled a drop of acid on her gown and made yet another small hole.

After nine acids, there was still no reaction, and Mary Lou was beginning to despair. Henrietta calmly said, "You have to be patient if you want to be a scientist." She dropped acid from another bottle on to the sample from the first petri dish, then the second but before she could continue there was a sizzling noise and green steam rose from the saucer.

"Ah ha," Henrietta said. "We have it."

"We do?" Mary Lou was plainly baffled.

"We have a reaction between tellalytou-ethyl and severistic acid." Henrietta walked over to the blackboard that took up most of one wall. On it she wrote:

$$\$6Fl10Zg^{1/4}b + J2LpGiGgGzW =$$

"Work out that equation, Mary Lou and tell me what you get."

Mary Lou stared blankly at the blackboard. "I haven't the first clue," she said. "I haven't done chemystery yet."

Henrietta crossed out letters, inserted symbols, manipulated fractions, moved numbers, and finally wrote:

$$D72GggxLxZ^{1/4}$$

"That's d-antipanti-quadra-sedium I think, but let's check."

Next to the blackboard was a large bookcase holding leather-bound tomes of great antiquity. Henrietta ran her forefinger along the gold printed titles, extracted a book, and laid it on a table. Flicking through the pages, she eventually found what she wanted. "Yes, that's the formula for d-antipanti-quadra-sedium. Now I will look up its uses."

She pulled out a heavy volume titled *Affirmation Ingredients: Their Utilization and Abutilization,* found the reference she wanted, and read out, "d-antipanti-quadra-sedium is an active ingredient in animopo-morphosis dissipation affirmations. Subjects transform into small fur-bearing mammals, the most common being cats, beaver, mink, and skunks. Subjects imbibing the same freshly made formula will end up together. For example, those transformed into beavers will inhabit the same lodge. This feature becomes important when one wants to remove people who hate each other."

Henrietta paused to say to Mary Lou, "Good, they are together so we won't have to search for them separately." She started to read again, "As subjects remain within a ten-mile radius of source, this is not a suitable hex to send a subject to the far ends of the earth. For this purpose, see f-antipanti-septum-sedium." She looked up with satisfaction. "There is a 0.25 probability that Matilda and Ciesta are skunks and that they are together and nearby. That should make it easy to find them." She stopped speaking and stared at the book. "Oh Jumping Jehoshapat, oh Wiley Wombats, what are we to do?"

"What is it?" Mary Lou said. "What's the matter?"

Henrietta read out, "Subjects under an animopo-morphosis dissipation hex must be reissipated within 5.45 days or they will lose their human qualities and become the creature forever."

"Brutal," Mary Lou said. "When is 5.45 days? I mean, what time on what day?"

"Well, today's Monday and it was about 10.30 a.m. when they left us, so work it out."

"I need a calculator," Mary Lou said.

"There's one in that drawer." Henrietta carried on reading. "If subjects are to be recovered in their former state they must be reissipated within five days. For each hour after that, one human quality is replaced by one feature of the animal form taken."

"In other words," Mary Lou said, "We have to find them and give them the counter-aff by 10:30 a.m. on Saturday and if we haven't done that by…" She pressed keys on the calculator, "by about 8 p.m. they will be skunks forever." She stared at Henrietta in horror.

"That's about the size of it," Henrietta said. "Now whatever you do, don't tell anyone about this time limitation. No one. Understand?"

"Why not?"

"Because if the faculty panic, that's all they'll do. They'll run round in circles saying 'Great Logos, spare me.' And then we'll never find Matilda and Ciesta." Henrietta closed the book with a bang. "Good work, Mary Lou. I'll see you at the faculty meeting in the morning."

15

How could I determine the number of ohms required to raise a column of black ewe's blood higher than a similar column of gotchamycin, Matilda wondered. Perhaps if she had a third variable, another column that would help the ewe's blood measure be more significant. Yes, that was it; she must measure a column of something else. But what? She opened her eyes and for a moment could not understand where she was. Then her memory jerked into gear—she was a skunk lying under a garage.

She could hear the sound of a rusty chainsaw but when she followed the noise she realised it was Ciesta snoring. "Ciesta, wake up." Matilda pushed at the sleeping ball of fur with her snout. "It's dusk and I think we should move from here as fast as we can."

"I'm hungry." Ciesta groaned as she stood up.

"Can't you think of anything else but your stomach?" Matilda said. "Let's get out of here and go back to the college."

They made their exit through the gap Doris dear had made to find that the garage opened on to a back lane. Ciesta headed off to the left.

"Not that way," Matilda said. "The college is west of here."

"This is west." Ciesta continued walking.

"No it's not. There's a glow in the sky over there so that must be west. The sun sets in the west in case you didn't know." Matilda turned right. She didn't care whether Ciesta followed, but eventually a panting noise indicated that Ciesta had run after her.

"Slow down a bit," Ciesta gasped. "I can't keep up with you."

After a few yards, the lane met a road. A child of about eight years was leaning on his bike licking an ice cream cone. Matilda turned back into the lane but Ciesta shuffled up to the boy and looked up at him hoping he would offer her a lick. "Urghh," the boy yelled. "A skunk." He threw down his ice-cream, straddled his bike and peddled away. Ciesta pounced on the cone and began to lick.

"Oh for Logos sake," Matilda said. "Don't you know enough to stay away from humans? They could kill us."

Ciesta stopped licking. "That's funny," she said. "This ice cream doesn't taste good; not good at all."

"Skunks don't eat ice cream." Matilda marched on determinedly to the next intersection. "Now if we can find out the name of these two roads we'll have some idea of where we are."

Ciesta peered up at the signpost. "I can't make out what it says, can you?"

"I think it's Larch but I'm not sure. I can see the other sign clearly: it's West 35th Avenue." Matilda sounded cheerful. "Now we know where we are. It's only a few miles to the college. Come on." Matilda began to cross the road and Ciesta followed. "I think we should stick to the lanes where possible," Matilda said. "Then we must devise a strategy for traversing the forest."

The university lay at the end of a peninsula and could only be reached by passing through a large swathe of reserved land covered with trees. Three main roads cut through it. There were also many trails and bridle paths but despite these, the forest was home to a variety of wildlife, including coyotes.

As they walked down the street, Matilda was careful to stay close to the hedges but Ciesta seemed to be unaware that she was not human and marched on the grass boulevard. "Come over here," Matilda said. "You can be seen under the street light."

"It's softer on my feet here, and one of them is sore." Ciesta lifted up one leg to examine her paw. Suddenly she wobbled, lost her balance and rolled into a parked car. The car's alarm set off with a shrill siren that made Ciesta stop and put her paws over her ears. A sound of a door opening and running feet followed.

Matilda took off. She bolted down the street, not caring what happened to Ciesta. In fact, she hoped that Ciesta would be caught or run over; anything. The woman was a menace, and quite likely to end up in a trap, taking Matilda with her. She made her way into the next lane and paused. By this time it was nearly dark, and in the ill-lit lane she could only make out the shapes of garbage pails, fences, and bushes. She hid behind an abandoned washing machine to regain her breath.

A shuffling noise grew louder. Before long Ciesta, with chest heaving, and in obvious distress, gyrated past as though drunk. She didn't see Matilda, who watched her with glee from her hideout. Matilda allowed her to proceed halfway along the lane and then followed silently. When Ciesta finally stopped she caught up with her.

"I thought…you'd…gone…without me," Ciesta managed to gasp.

"I will if you aren't more careful," Matilda said. "You don't seem to comprehend the danger we're in."

After Ciesta regained her breath they carried on, cautiously keeping to the sides of the lane and in the shadows of fences and hedges. Suddenly a large skunk stood before them, his eyes on Matilda.

"Now what do we do?" Matilda whispered.

"Nothing," Ciesta said. "He thinks we're his kin."

"How do you greet another skunk?" Matilda asked just as the large skunk gave a sort of leap and landed before her. Matilda stood still. The stranger gyrated before her, puffing out his fur and uttering deep grunts. Matilda remained motionless. The gyrations became more frenzied and violent. First he rotated one way, then the other. He turned his back on Matilda, lifted his tail and looked suggestively at her, first over one shoulder, then the other. After several minutes of this performance, he lay on his back and waved all fours in the same erratic motion.

"I think he fancies you." Ciesta laughed. "Your blonde stripe... and long snout must appeal to him. How long is it... since a male came on to you?"

"Oh, shut up," Matilda said. She was still rooted to one spot. "What do I do? How do I tell him I'm not interested?" She moved to one side. "Go away," she shouted to the male skunk. She turned tail and ran down the lane as fast as her four legs could carry her. The large skunk stood up. He stared after her but made no move to follow.

"Sorry," Ciesta said to it before she set off after Matilda. She looked behind her to see if the male was following, but he just stood there with his tail drooping.

In a couple of lanes further on, they came across another skunk, much smaller than the last, with wrinkled skin and a sparse, pink stripe to match pink-rimmed eyes. It cowered behind an old cardboard box filled with wood shavings.

"I've seen a lot of skunks in my time," Ciesta said, "but never one... as weird as that. Have you ever heard... of a skunk with a pink stripe?"

"Ciesta, is that you?" the pink skunk said in a timid little voice.

"Heavens to Betsy, who are you?" Ciesta asked in amazement.

"Octavia," said the pink skunk.

"What happened?" Matilda asked. "I'm Matilda, by the way."

"Yes, I made that assumption," Octavia said. "Well, the last thing I remember is that I was in my office with Prunella discussing objectives for the new course, Sorcery and its Antecedents. We were having tea. I was telling her about my cow's tail I recall. We were talking about talispersons. I didn't just bring up the subject. My first talisperson was black with one white hair. But it wasn't very effective. It came from a Hereford cow. Or was it Hertfordshire? Anyway, I changed it when—"

"Octavia, how did you come to be here?" Matilda interrupted.

"Here? Where are we?"

"You have assumed the form of a skunk. Do you realise that?"

"Oh yes," Octavia said. "Especially after Ciesta's remark about the weirdest skunk she's ever seen."

"I'm sorry," Ciesta said. "Of course I had no idea it was you. We have just met another skunk…that did a mating dance…in front of Matilda."

"Did he succeed?" Octavia asked.

"Certainly not," Matilda responded firmly. She repeated, "How did you come to be here?"

"Oh yes. Well I don't really know. I ate a piece of fudge and the next thing I knew I was here, in this lane. I hid for a while. Then I saw you two coming towards me. At least, I saw two skunks coming towards me, but I had no idea it was you until you spoke."

"What fudge?" Matilda said.

"Prunella offered me some fudge she'd bought in Grabville Market." Octavia tried to scratch her ear with a back paw but fell heavily with the effort. "I don't normally eat candy but it was getting late. At least, I think it was getting late. Oh dear, I can't remember what the time was."

"It doesn't matter," Matilda said. "We are all in the same position. We must plan a course of action."

"What plan?" Octavia said. "I can't think of anything we can do."

"We are making our way west, using the lanes that run parallel to West 35th Avenue. We want to get back to the college." Matilda told her. "We hope someone will find out we're skunks and come to find us."

"We can ask for help," Octavia said.

"No. We have found out that humans can't hear us even though we can hear each other," Matilda said. "We tried calling out to a woman but she didn't respond. I'm hoping that someone in the college will have the sense to realize who we are. What happened after we vanished?"

"At first, the faculty thought Mary Lou had made a dissipation aff, including a counter-aff that would promptly bring you back. So we were all impressed. No one had thought Mary Lou particularly bright, but an undergraduate student making a dissipation aff—imagine that! And you, Matilda, you really tutored her well. When other students find out, they'll all want you as a tutor. I know I would. I really needed help in my undergraduate years, especially with electronics. I never could understand the difference between a zat and a zut. You would—"

"If Mary Lou had made a counter-aff, I would be impressed too. As it is, we are skunks, and no one knows where we are, or even what we are. What did the dean say she was going to do?"

"The dean asked Henrietta and Mary Lou to find out what sort of dissipation aff it is. They are in the lab now, I expect."

"I trust she told the students to refrain from collecting any animal parts." Matilda sounded anxious.

"Oh yes. Don't worry. A total ban has been declared, even on the graduate students. They were pretty upset though, as some of them have comprehensives next week. I remember when I thought my comps were going to be delayed. There had been a fire in the lab and—"

Matilda interrupted. "We shall have to give them more time of course. Surely they realized why the ban is important?"

"Well, you know how stressed graduate students get. I remember myself holding on to my dissertation with both hands all the time. I was frightened someone would steal it, or a wind would come and blow the pages out of order. There was no limit to the horrors I dreamed up. But all in vain. I passed *cum laude*." Octavia chuckled. "It was a wonderful experiment—the best I've ever done. It has never been repeated, you know, and it should be, as it had great import on my levitation studies and could lead to…"

The three skunks walked in single file down the side of the lane. Octavia continued to prattle in her little voice but, as neither Matilda nor Ciesta could hear her, they did not respond.

Matilda paused for a moment to look around. We are an extraordinary sight, she thought. Barely recognisable as skunks—me with normal markings but a blonde stripe, one with pink markings and pink eyes, and the other looking like an overgrown marrow on legs with a red stripe. If we are ever found, no one will believe we are university faculty.

They walked on down the lane, hiding behind a bush when someone put on a light and came out with a garbage bag. After the man put it in the bin and closed the lid, he looked around sniffing. The three remained still until the man finally went back inside.

"That was a close shave," Octavia said. "I don't think I can cope with much more of this."

"We'll be safe in the forest," Matilda said. "From humans, anyway." She emerged from their hiding place to continue walking. "I don't understand how the aff ended up in some fudge. Surely someone made sure it was all secured?"

"Perhaps not," Ciesta said. "We all left the lecture hall together. As far as I know, everything was there as Mary Lou left it."

There was silence for a while; then Matilda said, "Octavia, you said you were sitting with Prunella? I wonder what happened?" But any suspicions she might have had were forgotten as they waited for traffic so they could cross a main road.

The next lane they entered was paved, unlike the litter-strewn by-ways they had so far used. Fences enclosed yards, garbage cans sat in containers, and garages were well built. There was nowhere for them to hide should they encounter danger so they hurried along as fast as they could.

To their astonishment, a young skunk suddenly appeared from nowhere. It looked at them for a moment, then turned and fled.

"Wait," called Matilda. "Wait. We won't hurt you."

The skunk stopped running and slowly faced them. "Who are you?" it said.

"Matilda, Ciesta and Octavia. Who are you?"

"Prunella," the skunk said. "Oh dear, oh dear, whatever have I done?"

"I don't know," Ciesta said. "What have you done?"

Prunella paused before saying, "I left my office unlocked while I went to do some copying. I had bought some fudge and ate a piece." She paused again. "The fudge was lying on my desk. Maybe someone tampered with it."

"Are you sure you didn't tamper with it yourself?" Matilda said.

"Of course not," Prunella said. "If I had put an aff in the fudge, I would hardly eat it myself, would I?"

"True, true. Anyway, now there are four of us in the same boat."

"So, what are you doing now?" Prunella demanded.

"We're making our way to the college," Matilda said.

"And how do you think anyone will recognise us?"

Matilda knew that tone. It was the same scathing way Prunella asked questions about exams. "Do you have another suggestion?"

"No."

"We will make our way to the college and hope that by the time we get there, Henrietta will have found out we're under an animopo-morphosis dissipation hex. Then they will come and look for us," Matilda said.

"And if they find us, then what? Does anyone know the counter-aff?" Prunella raised her tail so that it was higher than the others.

Always trying to assert herself, Matilda thought; even as a skunk. She said, "I believe I have the counter-aff in my filing cabinet but others, at least the more senior faculty, will also have it, I'm sure."

"I think we should go," Ciesta said. "It's still quite a ways."

The four skunks hurried along in the darkness.

16

When the dean arrived at the Faculty Club and saw Henrietta sitting in their usual corner, she inhaled deeply with relief. Henrietta must have finished and now knew the aff formula, or she would not be there. She ordered a gin and tonic and made her way over to greet Henrietta. "Am I pleased to see you! Your presence means you have finished, yes?" However, Henrietta's expression made her add, "Oh no, don't tell me."

"There's good news, yes, but there's bad news too, I'm afraid, dean. The good news is that we know it's an animopo-morphosis dissipation aff. I'm pretty sure that Matilda and Ciesta have taken on the form of skunks and that they are not far away. Somehow, Logos knows how, Mary Lou made d-antipanti-quadra-sedium."

The dean leaned back with a sigh. "That is good news. Well done, Henrietta." She sat forward again. "And the bad news?"

"They have to be given the counter-aff by 10:30 a.m. Saturday or they'll be skunks forever."

The dean and Henrietta stared at each other. Henrietta gave a hopeless shrug. "Even if we do find them, does anyone know the counter-aff?"

The dean sipped her gin thoughtfully. "We have two tasks: find two skunks and find a counter-aff. To start with, the problem of finding two skunks." She sighed. "I don't suppose skunks are difficult to find—there must be hundreds of them. I can't say I've ever searched for skunks before; they've just appeared when you don't want them. But even if we did find a couple of them, how would we know if they're Matilda and Ciesta?"

"I don't know. The description of the aff did say they would be within a 10-mile radius of source. And I suppose it would be up to them to attract our attention. Normal skunks would run away, I suppose. Or spray."

"Well, that limits our search area. Most of our 10-mile radius is out to sea. Skunks don't swim do they?" The dean raised her hand to the waiter and asked for another gin and tonic. "What will you have, Henrietta?"

"I think this situation calls for another Bloody Mary, thank you." Henrietta yawned. "I'm tired. I can't think straight. I don't know whether skunks can swim. I don't know much about them at all really. I know they stink and that's all." She yawned again.

"We must decide on a strategy. I suggest that we form search parties at the Faculty meeting in the morning. And then find out if anyone knows the counter-aff. Surely, in a school this size, someone will know. Or at least know how to find out."

"Whatever we do, don't let it be known that there is a time limit. You know how everyone goes into 'Great Logos spare me' mode." Henrietta downed her drink and stood up. "I need to sleep. I'll be thinking about it. Goodnight, dean."

After Mary Lou left the lab, she went to the student pub to see if any of her friends were there. The pub was full of students, but the only ones from the Academy of Sophistry were Julie and Andrea, who were isolated in one corner. As soon as students identified Sophists by the talispersons they wore suspended from chains around their necks, they steered clear of them. They had grown up with too many rumours about the evils of Sophistry, and students, despite their university education, are still prone to believe myths even when these are disproved by fact.

Mary Lou ordered a beer at the bar and took it across to join her friends. "Hey, Mary Lou," Julie said. "How are you doing? We heard you're in deep doo-doo."

"Yes, the aff I concocted for my exam made Matilda and Ciesta disappear, vamoose, goodbye." Mary Lou took a long swig of beer. "Trouble is, I don't know how to get them back."

"Awesome," Andrea said. "I wish I could make people vanish. There's quite a lot of people I'd like to see the back of."

"Where's your aff, Mary Lou?" Julie asked. "Can I have some?"

"It's all locked up in the faculty lab." Mary Lou dropped her voice to a whisper. "Except for one jar that's gone missing. Someone took it from the lecture hall."

"Are you serious?" Julie lowered her voice too. "We'll have to look out for people who don't show."

"Where do they go when they go?" Andrea asked.

"It's a dissipation aff of some sort."

"What's that?"

"Don't you remember the lecture on the three types of dissipation?" Mary Lou said. "I've had to work with Henrietta to find out what type mine is."

"I always fall asleep in Henrietta's lectures."

"Turned into animals, blown to the four winds, or disappeared into thin air," Mary Lou chanted. "We think Matilda and Ciesta are skunks."

Julie and Andrea stared at Mary Lou and burst into laughter. Tears ran down their cheeks as they snorted into their beer.

"It's not funny," Mary Lou said, but then she started to laugh too. Soon all three were so convulsed with mirth that they attracted attention from other students in the pub.

"Yes, it is. It's hysterical," Julie gasped. "Can you just imagine two skunks with mortarboards on?"

"I wonder if they know how to use their smell glands?" Andrea said. "They're all in the bum you know." At that they cracked up again. Then Mary Lou started to cry. The others stared at her in amazement.

"It's not funny," Mary Lou said again. "Do you realise what I've done? I've made two of my teachers disappear and they may never be found. I may as well have killed them."

"So you made a mistake. We all do," Andrea said.

"The faculty have to accept this sort of thing or else they can't teach here," Julie said as she handed Mary Lou a tissue. "Don't you remember when Zoe took the toes off her Cantrips teacher and she couldn't walk?"

"Trouble is," Andrea said, "if this gets out, the university might close the Academy. Then we won't be able to graduate."

"How do you know that?" Julie said.

"Everyone knows they want rid of us. Have done for years."

Julie glared at Andrea and reached out an arm to Mary Lou. "Come on, Mary Lou; it's not as bad as all that. They'll come back and somebody will reissipate them."

Mary Lou blew into a tissue and took a long swallow of beer. "Guess what? The faculty have the most amazing little creatures to help them in the lab. They're called lirrypoops, or lirrys for short. They make smells."

"Most animals smell," Julie said.

"No, I don't mean they smell," Mary Lou said. "I mean they make smells. Smells like chocolate or roses—anything."

"What good is that?" Andrea said.

"Well, Marvin made the smell of a skunk so that's how we knew they'd changed into skunks. They use them for all sorts of experiments."

"I think it's cruel to use animals in labs," Andrea said.

"You don't seem to mind collecting toe of frog or other bits," Mary Lou said.

"That's different."

"How?"

Andrea hesitated. "It's just different, that's all. All animals have predators. But to keep animals in cages to be used when, well whenever, is cruel. At least a frog hops around and has a life until we catch it."

"But then what does it do when it's lost its toe?" Mary Lou demanded. "I think that's cruel. Marvin seems quite happy. He's fed and looked after. And he does what comes naturally—makes smells."

"How do you know he's happy?" Andrea said. "Does he want to live in a cage? What's his natural habitat?"

"I don't know," Mary Lou said. "I think they breed them specially. Henrietta said they are difficult to metamorphasise."

"And you don't think it's cruel to keep animals in cages?" Andrea said.

"I hadn't really thought about it." Mary Lou turned to Julie. "What do you think?"

"Well, as long as they're fed and looked after, what's wrong with that?" Julie said.

"I think we all should try living in a cage and find out how it feels." Andrea's face had turned red.

They sat in silence for a while. "There's something I want to tell you," Mary Lou said. "I haven't told anyone else, so keep quiet. Promise?"

"Promise." Julie and Andrea leaned forward.

"I dropped the allspice on the floor and swept it up."

The others stared at her. Finally Julie said, "You spilled some powder and swept it up. So-o?"

"There must have been something on the floor that got into the spice. You see, I tasted my aff during my last trial and I'm still here, so there must be something in the spilled spice that's the active ingredient." Mary Lou stared at her friends, her face registering dismay. "I daren't tell Henrietta. I'm in enough trouble as it is."

"Didn't you say Henrietta has found out what the active ingredient is?"

"Yes," Mary Lou said. "But she thinks it's because of the spice I used. There's several sorts you see."

"Well then, she doesn't need to know you spilled it, does she? What difference would it make?" Andrea said.

"None, I suppose," Mary Lou said. She felt better for her friends' reactions.

The dean left the Faculty Club and strolled to her office to see if Herman was still there. This would be a good time to hex his jammer, she thought. It won't take long and it means one job out of the way. But then, thinking of a suitable aff required energy, and she wasn't sure she had any after all that had happened that day. First Mary Lou's disastrous exam, then trying to meet a deadline for her wrap-rage paper and being interrupted by Herman, and then by graduate students, but most of all, worrying about Matilda and Ciesta had worn her out. If they are skunks, she wondered, what are the chances of finding them? There must be hundreds of skunks out there. But they will surely show some initiative in trying to find the campus? They will, after all, still be able to think as humans. But perhaps instinct will override their thoughts. What would she do if she suddenly found she was a skunk? Depends where she ended up. The university was on the end of a peninsula and east of it is where the skunks must be, so all they had to do was head for the setting sun. What are the enemies of skunks? Humans of course, but what else? Dogs and coyotes and…they could be squashed by a car, the dean thought with horror. If so, how would we ever know?

The dean was preoccupied with the image of identifying a flattened skunk as Matilda when she reached her office. Herman should have gone home hours ago but he was still there, obviously waiting to see if she would return. His desk in her outer office was littered with tiny screws, coloured wire, resistors, capacitors, and a set of small screwdrivers. An instrument, similar in size to a TV remote, lay to one side with its electrical innards exposed. The dean stared at it with as much understanding as when she looked inside a computer; that is, with wonder.

"Right," she said, "the lab's free so let's go and hex your instrument."

Herman looked up with a big smile. He quickly put the case on the remote and screwed it down. "Fantassimo," he said. "Here it is, all ready. Let me explain what these knobs do."

"Not now, Herman. I'm tired and I need to concentrate on the aff as we walk over." The dean knew that he would become intense in his explanation and, remembering the chart, she shuddered at the thought of hearing about JIM Beams, wavelengths, diodes, and the rest.

"Why can't we do it here?" Herman asked.

"You know very well that the atmospheric environcouls are too high here and interfere with affs. The lab is just right. I have them adjusted every year."

The dean strode off, walking so fast that even Herman's long legs had trouble keeping up with her. She concentrated on the aff she was to intone. It had to be something more than the usual doggerel, something more sophisticated, something with eminence so that its effect would last. Hmm.

As usual, Herman fell up the stairs. There was something about his lack of coordination that made his upper body out of sync with his legs. The dean ignored the clatter, opened the lab and looked around for an empty bench. She chose one in a corner as far away as possible from potential malignant influences.

"Put it on here," she commanded Herman. "And then sit over there and don't interrupt. I need to think." She closed her eyes for a few minutes. Just as Herman shifted restlessly on his stool, she rubbed her talisperson, pointed it at the jammer, raised her other arm, and chanted like a Shakespearean actor:

Shall I compare you to a toy remote?
You are more potent and more splendid.
Panda, roebuck, Billy goat
Herman's jammer! – work as he intended.

The dean lowered her arms. "There. That should do it."

Herman shuffled across the lab to retrieve his jammer. He seemed disappointed.

"What's the matter?" the dean asked.

"Why Billy goat?"

"Why not?"

"It doesn't make sense." Herman pulled at his tee-shirt and glowered.

"Chanting affs don't have to." The dean wanted to go home. "All it means, Herman, is that your jammer is more splendid than a panda, a roebuck, or a Billy goat."

"Oh." He hesitated. "Well, thank you, dean. I'll try it out tomorrow. It's too late tonight."

17

"I'm getting tired," Octavia moaned. "Can't we have a rest?"

"So am I," Ciesta said. "I haven't walked...so far...for a long time." She stopped to pant.

I bet you haven't, Matilda thought. "Another block or two and we'll be in the forest," she said. "We'll rest there when we're well away from people." It occurred to her that she had taken charge and that she enjoyed the feeling. Before her nose let her down, she had been quite assertive, but after she'd overheard someone call her "that twitchy bitch" she had shrunk from taking on authority; how could anyone respect a leader with a tremulous nose?

The four skunks entered the last lane before the forest. It was more rural than the previous lanes, with large shrubs bordering a muddy cart track. Behind one shrub they found an open compost heap on which someone had recently emptied a pile of carrot peelings, outer lettuce leaves, apple cores, and withered celery. Octavia took one end of a celery stalk just as Ciesta took the other. They began to tug. Ciesta, being the heaviest, backed away pulling hard. Octavia clung on and was dragged across the compost heap on to a lawn. Ciesta increased her speed and then suddenly let go so that Octavia fell backwards. Ciesta ran off with her prize.

Octavia, panting, called out, "Ciesta, that's mine. I'm the senior."

"The skunk supremo, eh?" Ciesta said through her munching.

"Octavia, come back here. There's plenty more celery," Matilda called from the compost heap.

"That's not the point," Octavia said. "Ciesta had no right to take my celery."

"Ciesta, did you take Octavia's celery?" Matilda said.

"It wasn't hers. I had just as...much right to it," Ciesta said.

Matilda picked up a celery stick, dropped it in front of Octavia and said, "Here. Have this one."

"No," Octavia said. "I want the one I found."

"Ciesta's eaten it. Have this one instead."

"Shan't," Octavia said, and lay down on the grass.

Matilda carried on chewing and ignored Octavia. Finally she said, "Come on everyone, finish up. We need to get going."

Octavia refused to get up.

"Ciesta, would you please apologize to Octavia so we can carry on," Matilda said firmly.

"Oh all right. I'm sorry I took your celery, Octavia. I won't do it again," Ciesta said in a sing-song voice.

Octavia did not answer but got to her feet.

They carried on walking with Ciesta keeping her distance from Octavia. She knew very well that she would never have got away with upsetting her when they were in their normal form, or Octavia would have performed one of her famous malicious hexes—despite the rule that they were not to practice Sophistry on each other. But as Octavia's short-term memory was notoriously poor, Ciesta was sure she would not retaliate later, as the incident would be forgotten.

"There's the forest ahead," Matilda said. "Keep going Octavia, we're nearly there. Then we'll find a sheltered spot for a rest."

As they approached the last house on the lane, frenzied barking broke the silence. A Border Collie ran out from the garden. The white ruff of his black and white coat stood out in the gloom; so did his teeth. When he saw the skunks, he took the stance a sheepdog takes when about to herd a flock of sheep—alert, head down, advancing deliberately.

"Oh, oh," Octavia cried. "I'm terrified of dogs.

The Collie began, very slowly, to circle behind them. Prunella made a run for it. The dog ran faster, placed itself in front of her, and took the 'down' position.

"You three go over there by that garbage can," Matilda said. "I'll handle this."

Prunella backed away to join Ciesta and Octavia beside the garbage can. Matilda advanced upon the dog. He fixed his eyes on her as he put his head down and remained motionless. Matilda stomped her front feet, raised her tail and walked, stiff legged, towards him. She stopped when she was about four feet away, turned her back towards him, and sprayed. The dog gave a yelp, rubbed his face back and forth on the ground, and then bolted for home.

"Wow," said Prunella.

"Good for you, Matilda. However did you do that?" Ciesta asked.

"I just sort of, well, I don't quite know how to describe it." Matilda hesitated. "As a matter of fact, I farted at it."

"Can we all do that?" Octavia asked.

"I guess so," Prunella said. "But once you've done it, I believe it takes 24 hours to re-fill, so to speak."

"If that's the case, I'm out of the running as a protector," Matilda said. "Someone else will have to do it if we meet a coyote or something."

"I don't think I would know how," Ciesta said.

Matilda chuckled. "You'll know how. It just came naturally."

In a few minutes they were in the safety of the forest where, without the glow of streetlights, it was even darker than before. They found themselves on a footpath and followed it until they reached a small stream. They drank thirstily.

"We can rest here for a while but we should find a safe place to hide before daylight," Matilda said. "If we can reach the golf course we could hide under the hut where they keep the lawnmowers and things. I know it is off the ground because I once inadvertently putted a ball under it. I wonder if that ball is still there?"

"If it is, how will you carry it?" Prunella asked her.

"How much further is the golf course?" Octavia twittered. "I don't think I can walk much more."

"Soak your paws in the stream," Matilda said. "We'll rest here for a short time but then we really must carry on."

They curled up; each huddled close to a tree. All but Prunella prepared to sleep. Her mind was too busy wondering if there was some way she could get rid of the others and reissipate herself. If she ran off and reached the college before them, there was no guarantee anyone would know who she was. And it was Matilda who had the counter-aff. What if no one else did? No, there was nothing for it but to stay with the others and see what she could do when they were back. She cursed herself for eating the piece of fudge; how could she have been so stupid? I'll never eat fudge again for as long as I live, she vowed.

Matilda scratched herself vigorously. Her glands were itchy after their discharge at the dog. Although her eyes were closed, her mind was also busy. Octavia said she ate a piece of Prunella's fudge. Prunella was present at the time so she must have seen the effect. Why didn't she go for help? Why would she eat the fudge too when she'd seen what happened? That was the most puzzling part.

Matilda uncurled for a stretch, and after about thirty minutes she poked the other three and they set off once more. Octavia walked stiffly with a limp in her rear right leg that made her unstable and ready to fall. Matilda walked beside her and made encouraging remarks: "Nearly there, Octavia," "Keep going, not much further now," "You can have a good rest when we are safe."

"Do you think a coyote will attack us?" Octavia was clearly shaken by the encounter with the sheepdog.

"They do live here but we know how to deal with them, so I don't think there's any danger," Matilda reassured her.

Prunella, lost in thought, walked ahead. She was so intent that it was a few minutes before she realized she was walking on soft grass.

"We're here," she called. "We're at the golf course. The others hurried to join her. "Where's the clubhouse?" Octavia asked.

"Keep walking straight," Matilda said. She was the only one who played golf so she knew the course. "We'll be there in a minute. It's just beyond those trees."

Dawn was beginning to break when they reached a cluster of buildings. Matilda led them to the groundsman's shed where, as she remembered, there was a crawl space underneath. "There's my ball," Matilda cried with satisfaction as she nosed at it with her long snout.

The ground was dry with soft earth. Making little hollows with their paws, they each curled up and fell fast asleep.

18

The day after Mary Lou's disastrous examination, the Faculty of Sophistry assembled promptly to hear about the progress, or lack of it, in recovering its members. Henrietta, looking rather smug, stood at the podium. Mary Lou, sitting on a chair to one side of the stage, wriggled uncomfortably and played with her fingers. Everyone was waiting for the dean to come in and open the proceedings. She was late. When she did arrive, she looked around anxiously before saying, "Has anyone seen Octavia?"

Everyone shook her head. "I can't understand it," the dean said. "I arranged to meet her an hour ago but she is nowhere to be seen. Her propellant is here, so she must have arrived."

"Have you checked her office?" someone asked.

"Of course. That's how I know her propellant is there," the dean said. "Her door was unlocked, so she must be here. The funny thing is that dirty teacups were still laid out. That's most unlike Octavia. She always washes up and tidies her office before she leaves for the day."

"Perhaps she had business elsewhere on campus?" someone suggested.

"She would have phoned or left me a note if she had been called away," the dean said. There was silence for a while. "Another odd thing is that there was a box of fudge with only one piece in it, on her desk. I know she doesn't eat candy. There were two teacups, so someone must have been with her."

Henrietta was looking thoughtful. "I think I should tell you that when Mary Lou and I came here yesterday to pick up her equipment, one jar of brew was missing."

The dean turned to Henrietta. "Why on earth didn't you tell us before?"

"I saw no point in alarming you," Henrietta said stiffly. "Besides, what could you have done?"

"Nothing, I suppose, except keep on the alert," the dean said. "Is there anyone else missing?"

"Yes. Prunella," a young Sophist said.

"Would you go to her office and see if she is there? She may have forgotten about this meeting," the dean asked her. "Meanwhile, let us proceed. Henrietta, would you tell us about your progress?"

Henrietta cleared her throat. "Mary Lou and I began by presenting a lirry with her ingredients, one at a time. It sneezed at the allspice which made me suspect that it was the active constituent. When presented with the entire brew, the lirry emitted the smell of…" Henrietta paused for effect, "a skunk."

The faculty gasped and turned to each other to comment. Henrietta raised her hand. "As I was certain that the aff lay in the allspice that Mary Lou used, I prepared three types of separating gel and tested each with different acids. You may see data about the whole experiment if you wish. I will just give you the outcome."

"Thank Logos," came clearly from the back of the lecture hall. The dean turned round to glare.

Henrietta walked over to the blackboard. "There was a reaction between tellalytou-ethyl and severistic acid. So we had $6Fl10Zg^{1/4}b + J2LpGiGgGzW$." She wrote the equation on the blackboard. "Which works out to be $D72GggxLxZ.^{1/4}$ That's d-antipanti-quadra-sedium, as you know."

At that moment, the young Sophist returned from searching for Prunella. "She isn't there, but her propellant is. She also has fudge in her office, piled on a saucer."

"How odd," the dean said. "We'll deal with that later. Carry on, Henrietta."

"d-antipanti-quadra-sedium is the active ingredient in animopomorphosis dissipation affs. Subjects turn into small, fur-bearing animals, including skunks."

Henrietta waved an arm triumphantly. "I think we can safely say that Matilda and Ciesta have taken on the form of skunks. Are there any questions?"

"Well done, Henrietta," the dean said. "Now the main question is how to recover them. And then, when we've found them, give them the counter-aff. Does anyone know of an antidote?"

There was silence. One studious looking assistant professor said, "I believe someone in Utrecht is working on this problem. I will look up the reference and contact her, if you like."

"Thank you. That would be most helpful. Perhaps you could also do a literature search." The dean looked around. "Anyone else know the antidote? No? Very well, let's tackle the problem of finding them. Henrietta?"

"My reference indicated that an animopo-morphic dissipation hex sends a subject no further than within a ten mile radius and that all subjects taking the same aff at the same time will be together," Henrietta said. "I was thinking that if a volunteer took the aff and joined the others, she could be instructed to lead them to a pre-ordained meeting place. I doubt if they are far away."

"Why don't we send out search parties if they are near by?" someone said.

"Yes, we could do that," the dean said. "But let us consider Henrietta's idea. Are there any volunteers?" No one spoke. Gradually, everyone's gaze fixed on Mary Lou who shrank into her chair.

The dean and Henrietta turned to Mary Lou without saying anything. They just stared.

"Me?" Mary Lou said in alarm. "I don't want to turn into a skunk."

"This is, after all, your responsibility, Mary Lou," the dean said firmly. "I think it only just that you take your own brew."

"I'll go and get some," Henrietta said. She left the lecture hall by the back door.

"While we are waiting for Henrietta, let us consider the disappearance of Octavia and Prunella. Does anyone have any ideas?" the dean asked.

"Do you think that it's conceivable that they could have taken the brew? If so, how?" someone said.

"Henrietta said that a jar was missing from the stage when you went to collect them. Is that right, Mary Lou?"

"Yes." Mary Lou tried to bring her mind back to the lecture hall from a daydream about being a skunk in a meadow with a cougar in pursuit. "There were twelve jars when Matilda and I counted them but only eleven when Henrietta and I fetched them."

"I think we should assume that Octavia and Prunella have also turned into skunks until proven otherwise," the dean said. "So we are now searching for four skunks. I hope that Henrietta is right and they're together."

The back door to the stage opened and Henrietta appeared carrying two jars of Mary Lou's brew and a spoon. Mary Lou wanted to rush out of the room, but fear glued her to her chair.

"When you find them, Mary Lou, you are to inform them of our progress and lead them to the West door of this building. Someone will always be at that door waiting for you. We will also send out search parties," the dean said.

Henrietta walked over to Mary Lou. She unscrewed the lid of one jar, dipped in the spoon and handed it to Mary Lou. "Take this," she said.

With a trembling hand, Mary Lou took the spoon and placed it in her mouth.

"My god, what a dreadful smell of skunk." The loud male voice woke up Matilda. She opened her eyes and rolled over so that she could peer out from under the groundsman's shed. Blinded by sunlight she could see nothing for a few seconds and then, as her eyes adjusted, she saw two pairs of legs and a golf cart.

"I think it's coming from under that hut," a female voice said. "We better let Fred know."

Matilda felt a body beside her. "Is that Doris dear again?" Celia said.

"I don't know what her name is but she has the same motive as Doris dear," Matilda said. "That is, to get rid of us."

"Just when we're so near the college," Ciesta said.

By this time, Prunella had woken up too. "What's happening?"

"Someone has smelled us, that's all," Matilda told her. "Don't worry. Nothing's going to happen straight away. Go back to sleep. We'll leave here as soon as it's dark." She returned to her hollow and curled up.

19

Herman arrived in his office early, eager to test the jammer. If his calculations were correct, and he was sure they were, one button altered the beam wavelength, another the beam colour, and a third, the radius. Pressing each button would register the JIU, the Jamming Intensity Unit, in the small window of the jammer. Once he had estimated the distance between himself and the engine he wished to switch off, he could adjust the other readings to produce a JIU of 0.111111, the optimal figure.

The major problem was in estimating the radius from him to the engine. If he was stationary and the engine was moving, the distance would vary over time. He hadn't quite solved this problem although he had been working on it. There were two spare conduits in the jammer to allow for variables he hadn't thought of. He might have to use one to estimate the Doppler effect[8], but his first trial was to be on an engine that was operating and stationary.

The dean was in a meeting and the secretary out, so he was on his own in the suite of rooms that comprised 'the dean's office.' The main doors of the suite opened into a waiting room, and beyond that were two small offices, one for Herman and one for the secretary. Beyond those lay the dean's spacious room. When the dean first took up her position, she installed a large and colourful fish tank in the waiting room, taking the lead from her optician. She took more interest in it than Herman did, although it was his responsibility to clean the tank when necessary and to feed the fish daily. The latest addition to the tank was an elephantnose. It's black and silver body, its forked tail, and its long pointed nose fascinated the dean, who had named it 'Fetish.' Whenever she entered the office she

---

8   Doppler effect: an increase (or decrease) in the frequency of sound, light, or other waves as the source and observer move towards (or away from) each other.

would peer into the tank and make clucking noises. Herman kept pointing out that fish don't cluck, but she ignored him.

Herman, trying to visualise ten yards, carefully counted ten strides from the fish tank. He turned to point the jammer, keyed in 'ten,' adjusted the wavelength and the colour and yes, the JIU registered 0.111111. Fantassimo, he thought, we're in business; now to try it outside.

Across the road, at the newly built Centre for Post-Graduate Studies, a backhoe noisily churned up earth to prepare for a garden. Herman stopped to admire the lines of the modern pink concrete building and wondered why the dean hated it so much. Equidistant narrow buttresses gave the impression of reaching to the sky; reaching and searching for knowledge, Herman liked to imagine. The wide, four-storey block was flanked by two round towers that housed staircases, but it was the entrance that fascinated Herman. Built on the lines of an English stately home, it was completely out of keeping with the building both in size and in architectural design. The wall above the portico was free of windows, but metal bars protruded from it as though waiting to support something.

Herman focused on the backhoe. Although its bucket moved up and down, the rest of it was stationary. A perfect sample for his first test. And he hardly had to move from his own doorway that he reckoned was 50 yards away. He keyed in '50,' adjusted the other readings, got a JIU of 0.111111, directed the beam at the backhoe, and pressed the 'start' button.

The excavator's engine coughed, whirred, and stopped. Herman could see the operator turn a key but nothing happened. After a few tries the operator climbed out of her cab and walked away.

It was then that Herman noticed the helicopter. Or, to be more exact, he noticed an enormous wooden object dangling from the end of a cable attached to a slowly descending silent helicopter whose propellers rotated uselessly. As the object neared the ground Herman realized it was a shield bearing a coat-of-arms.

Herman, now surrounded by students and staff, watched helplessly as the shield reached the road. For a moment it balanced upright on its pointed end before toppling backwards and landing with an ominous crack. Large pieces of what had been an impressive and colourful coat-of-arms lay on the tarmac. The helicopter, relieved of its load, drifted sideways to come to rest on top of one of the towers like a stork settling into its nest.

A blue-tinted woman in very high heels cried, "My shield! Look what's happened to my shield!" She rushed towards the remnants followed by a man Herman recognised as the Chancellor.

"Never mind the bloody shield," someone shouted, "what about the pilot?"

Up on the tower a small figure could be seen waving from the helicopter.

"I'll phone the fire department," a student said, and pulled out his cell phone.

Most of the crowd moved to stand below the tower while Herman and a few others gathered round the Chancellor and the well-dressed woman. The Chancellor was saying, "Never mind, Lady Otterbrook, I'm sure it can be replaced."

"But it's a coat-of-arms I had designed specially. To remember my dear Basil." Lady Otterbrook dabbed her eyes with a lace handkerchief. "Now look at it."

Two griffins rampant lay with arms outstretched as though to hold the red and yellow shield that had escaped their clutches. One griffin's head had become partially detached from its body so that its lolling tongue now pointed upwards in what Herman thought was a remarkably obscene gesture.

A waving green banner, that had been the base of the coat-of-arms, was still intact. It bore the motto, *Doctorem Philosophiae Non Gradus Anus Rodentum* in gothic script.

"Oh dear," said an untidy, white-haired man in cords. "I think there's been some mistake."

"What makes you say that, Doctor Flavus?" the Chancellor asked.

"You definitely do not want to erect this; definitely not." The professor shook his head.

"Why not?" Lady Otterbrook demanded.

The professor coughed. "Are you sure you want it to read, 'A Ph.D is not worth a rat's ass'?"

"What?" Both Lady Otterbrook and the Chancellor stared at each other.

Lady Otterbrook rooted in her handbag and pulled out a piece of paper. "It was meant to say, *Non Scholae Sed Vitae Discimus*. That means 'We do not learn for school but for life.'"

"It's perhaps a good thing it did crash to the ground," the Chancellor said. "Now come with me, Lady Otterbrook, and I'll find you a cup of coffee while I set the wheels in motion to investigate this accident. And," he added grimly, "find out who altered the motto. It sounds like an engineering prank."

Herman slunk back to his office feeling guilty and confused. The jammer had worked, that was certain, but why was the helicopter affected? It was plain bad luck that it had been there at the time but it wasn't in his 50 yard radius. Then it dawned on him; it wasn't the radius he had calculated but the hemisphere. That meant that everything above him would be affected. He hadn't thought of that.

He settled down happily to recalibrate the jammer.

20

Mary Lou stood on the lecture hall stage with a spoon sticking out of her mouth. She was so entranced with the delicious taste of her brew that it was a few moments before she realized that she was still there, that she had not vanished.

Henrietta said, "Perhaps I didn't give you enough. Here, give me the spoon." She scooped more brew out of the jar and handed it to Mary Lou.

Mary Lou's tongue extended to lick off the contents of the spoon. Her mouth was aglow with delightful sensations as if she had just feasted on gourmet stuffed mushrooms, shrimp cocktail and Pavlova cake. She became aware that as soon as she thought of a food, her mouth provided the taste of it. She imagined Belgian milk chocolate. Her mouth responded. She thought of fish and chips. She licked imaginary salt off her lips.

Before she could think of more favourite foods, Henrietta said, "This is the jar that we opened for our experiments. Its effect seems to have worn off. I wonder if contact with air has rendered it impotent?"

"Try an unopened jar," the dean said.

The professors, who until then, had been sitting in suspenseful silence as they waited for Mary Lou to vanish, now began to murmur amongst themselves.

Henrietta broke the seal of a fresh jar, took the spoon from Mary Lou, dipped it and handed it back. Mary Lou opened her mouth eagerly. There were the sensations again. She closed her eyes and thought of papayas, peaches, fresh picked strawberries, oranges warmed by the sun, pineapple and coconut smoothies. In ecstasy she let out a long, "Mmmm…" and opened her eyes.

Henrietta stared at her in annoyance. "What are you doing?" she said. "Why are you still here?"

"Oh taste that," Mary Lou licked her lips. "It does, as I said, affect the taste buds. It gives you the taste of any food you think of. Try it."

Henrietta tentatively dipped a long fingernail into the brew and sucked it. "Chicken à la Kiev," she said, "with asparagus, followed by crème caramel."

"Let me try." The dean followed suit. The three on the stage were so lost in delicious tastes that they did not respond to the rest of the faculty who wanted to know what was going on. Eventually, one teacher strode on to the stage, grabbed a jar from Henrietta and took it down to the others. Before long a crowd of black clad figures was pushing and elbowing for a chance to dip a finger into the brew. The room sang with 'mmm's as if it had been invaded by a swarm of humming bees.

The rapturous look left Henrietta's face. "The taste sensation seems to only last about ten minutes, but it's miraculous while it does." She looked at Mary Lou, who had also recovered. "Whatever you did, Mary Lou, you seem to have discovered something important. It is unfortunate that its first effect is that of a dissipation aff."

"Despite the success of Mary Lou's brew as a taste enhancer," the dean said, "we are still left with the problem of recovering Matilda and Ciesta, and, possibly, Octavia and Prunella."

"True," Henrietta said. "But I think Mary Lou should receive credit for a remarkable achievement."

"Her achievement will be even more remarkable if she can recover four of our faculty," the dean said. "My suggestion is that we form search parties and sweep the area around here, particularly to the east, in the forest."

"I have two lectures to give this afternoon," someone said.

"Yes, and I have a three-hour lab," another teacher said.

"We are all busy, I know." The dean walked to and fro on the stage, thinking. She was torn between telling the faculty about the time limit, and keeping silent. Henrietta was right: they probably would panic. On the other hand, she didn't want them to think they could postpone action indefinitely. But then, skunks are nocturnal, and they would more easily be found in the evening. She decided to give the faculty the afternoon to conduct their usual business and then start the search. "Let us meet here at 4:30 and organize ourselves then. We shall have a chance to catch up on our work and still be left with enough daylight. Is that agreeable?"

Many of the faculty nodded as they prepared to leave. "Before you go," the dean added, "I must stress the importance of keeping this incident to ourselves. This is all the university needs to get rid of us. If it comes out or, Logos help us, if the press finds out, we will all be looking for other jobs."

Henrietta said to Mary Lou, "You better rescue your two jars of brew. They are your work." She lowered her voice to a whisper. "You must watch out that no one steals your recipe or claims your work as theirs. It happens to students. I will keep your remaining nine jars and your ingredients locked up until you are ready to collect them." She patted Mary Lou on the arm. "We may make a Sophist out of you yet!"

Mary Lou tried to smile.

"Be here at 4:30, Mary Lou," the dean called out as she left.

Mary Lou found her two jars, now almost empty, and set off for the cafeteria to meet Julie.

The dean took Henrietta aside. "Right, that's set the search going. Now, what about the counter-aff?"

"Let's hope the University of Utrecht knows it. Or that someone has published it somewhere."

"The hardest thing is the waiting."

"It's only Tuesday, dean. We still have three whole days." Henrietta smiled. "And nights."

The dean returned to her office. As usual she walked over to the fish tank to cluck at Fetish, but instead of a cluck she let out a gasp of horror. Fetish, and all the other fish, were floating belly up, decidedly lifeless. The dean compressed her lips. "Herman," she yelled. "Come here."

Herman appeared out of his office. The dean stood by the tank and pointed. "Have you been trying out your jammer on my fish tank?"

"No, dean, of course not." Herman came forward and peered into the tank. "Someone must have switched off the heater."

"It was working when I came in this morning."

"Yes."

The dean glared at Herman. "Well?"

Herman licked his lips. "I did point the jammer, yes, but I was only estimating the distance. It wasn't on. I swear it."

"Well it obviously switched off the heater. The power's still on so it wasn't a power outage." The dean continued through tight lips, "Get rid of those corpses and clean out that tank. And," she added as she stomped into her office, "keep out of my sight."

She slammed her briefcase down on her desk. She was in no mood to do anything useful. Suddenly her attention was attracted to something going on outside the window. A large crowd surrounded an enormous fire truck with its red lights flashing. Everyone, with craned necks, watched a fireman escort a man down an extended ladder from the tower on which a helicopter nestled. The dean stared in amazement. Then—this was Herman's doing, she realised. Her next thought was that if people figured out that this was due to an action of her personal assistant, she could kiss her school goodbye.

She bellowed, "Herman."

Herman did not appear. She yelled again before flinging open her door and marching into his office. Herman had wisely taken off.

21

Mary Lou found Julie and Andrea wandering round the food counters in the student cafeteria trying to decide what to eat. As they ate lunch there every day, they were bored with the selection. Finally Andrea and Julie each chose a slice of rather dried up pizza and a salad, and Mary Lou, Chinese food. They looked for seats in the quieter section near the back where the nerds claimed tables for most of the day by spreading books and folders over them. As there were no empty seats, they piled up the books on one unoccupied table and sat down.

"Guess what?" Mary Lou said. "My brew doesn't make people disappear any more. I was supposed to dissipate and lead deMeow and Sands back, but when I tasted my potion, well…" Mary Lou placed her jars on the table. "That pizza looks really dry. What would you like it to be?"

"Sushi. California rolls," Julie said.

"Turkey, roast potatoes, and all the trimmings," Andrea said.

"Okay." Mary Lou opened a jar. "Dip your fork into that and think of those foods." She sat back to watch her friends' faces change from scepticism to rapture.

"Hey, Mary Lou," Andrea said with her mouth full. "This is a miracle! It tastes like plum chutney but it has magic in it." She looked at Mary Lou admiringly. "It's made my pizza taste just like a Thanksgiving dinner."

"And mine tastes like sushi even though I know it isn't. Wow," Julie said.

Mary Lou dipped her knife into the brew and spread the pink jelly over her dried up chop suey. "I want this to be barbecued salmon, baked potato with sour cream and chives, and fresh okra." She took a forkful, closed her eyes and savoured the delicious taste of the foods she thought of.

"Mary Lou, if you can make this you could sell it for a fortune," Andrea said. "You could go into business."

"Really?" Mary Lou's eyes widened. "That would solve a lot of my problems. But I don't know anything about setting up a business."

"You could take courses in business management," Julie said.

A stern looking young woman came up to them. "This is my table. Those are my books you moved."

"You weren't here," Andrea said. "You know you're not allowed to use tables in here unless you're eating."

The woman persisted. "You had no business touching my things. Move. I want to sit down."

"Can either of you Sophists do something with her?" Andrea asked Mary Lou and Julie.

"Certainly." Julie fingered her talisperson and stood up.

The young woman hurriedly said, "Okay. Okay," picked up her books and moved away.

The three students finished their lunch in peace. They chatted more about the prospect of marketing Mary Lou's brew. "I can't even think of what to do with it until the professors are found," Mary Lou said. "I have to go to another faculty meeting at 4:30. They're going to organize search parties."

"Why don't we three look for them now?" Julie said. "We can skip our lab."

"It would be awesome if we found them," Andrea said. "Where are they likely to be?"

"In the forest probably. They'll be within a ten-mile radius of where they disappeared. Most of that is on campus or out to sea so they're most likely to the east."

"Let's take our propellants and search the forest."

"Great idea," Julie said. "How are we going to do it?"

"I've got a map somewhere. Come up to my room," Andrea said.

They headed for the dorm. Andrea found the map and opened it. "Here: you do this section, Mary Lou, and you do this bit, Julie, and I'll do this. We'll meet at the golf club."

"What if one of us finds them?" Mary Lou asked.

"Lead them to the golf club, then we can all escort them on to campus."

"What shall we do? Call out?" Julie said. "What if they can't hear us?"

"Henrietta said they're supposed to be able to hear us even though we may not be able to hear them," Mary Lou told them. "Anyway, you should smell them before you see them."

"And there's two together, right?"

"Well, there may be four. Dr. Rale and Peidmore aren't around. They may have got hold of the missing jar of brew," Mary Lou said. "Burghul expects they'll identify themselves somehow." I sure hope they do, Mary Lou thought. She wanted to tell the others about the time limit but she had been sworn to secrecy. She also wanted to talk about how badly she felt about turning her teachers into skunks but, like other students, they considered these events par for the course.

The three students found their propellants and left together. After doing a few Guyan mudra exercises, Mary Lou managed to steer behind the others and she flew to the edge of the forest without incident. They separated to follow their assigned routes and Mary Lou, much to her surprise, liked following forest paths close to the ground. She called out, "Matilda deMeow, Ciesta Sands," every few minutes, stopped to listen, and re-engaged the forsometer easily.

She wanted to think about the wonder of her brew and about Andrea's suggestion that she market it. If she could produce her brew in bulk she would be financially independent and could leave the School of Sophistry. She suddenly had a thought: she must rescue the jar of allspice, as that obviously held the secret. Or did it? Was whatever she swept off the floor responsible for the dissipation property, or did it give the enhanced taste? She thought she had made a taste enhancer, yes, but not one with such miraculous properties. Perhaps it was the unknown ingredient that had made it magical.

She was so engrossed in her thoughts she nose-dived and nearly crashed. She would have to think about it later; now she must concentrate on where she was going.

She reached a junction, where she stopped to recall the map. Andrea's instructions had been to turn left and the path would shortly lead out of the forest to a road. She had to propel down that for about one hundred yards before re-entering the forest. When the road appeared, she knew she was on the right track.

Shortly after re-entering the forest, she reached a stream. Was it her imagination or could she smell skunk? She searched through the bushes for a while but as there was no movement or other sign of life she set off once more. *Even if we don't find them, at least I'll be able to tell the faculty that I tried,* she thought. *Then they can leave this area out of their search.*

Andrea and Julie reached the clubhouse before Mary Lou and were inside drinking juice when she arrived. "Any luck?" she asked. The others shook their heads. "I thought I smelled skunk once but I didn't see anything." She ordered a large orange juice and when it was served, she said, "Let's drink these outside. In the sun." They sat on the deck overlooking the first green and across to the groundsman's hut. A light breeze blew their way and once again Mary Lou thought she could smell skunk. "They couldn't be here by any chance?" she said. As there was no one else on the deck, she leaned over the rail between wooden boxes of brightly coloured primulas and shouted, "Matilda deMeow, Ciesta Sands, Matilda deMeow, Ciesta Sands," several times, then sat down.

Under the hut Matilda dreamed that someone was calling her. She woke up. There was the voice again. It was calling her. She nuzzled the others. "Wake up. Wake up. I think we've been found."

With some hesitation, she emerged from under the hut, prepared to retreat at the first sign of danger. Slowly, the others joined her. When her eyes were accustomed to the light, she saw Mary Lou sitting on the deck of the clubhouse.

"Quick," she said. "There's Mary Lou." She hurried across the grass.

"What's that awful stink?" Julie held her nose.

"Skunk," Mary Lou replied. She jumped up to look over the railing and saw four skunks coming towards her. "We've found them," she shouted. "There they are!"

They rushed through the café and across the grass towards the skunks. The three students stood in front of them not knowing what to say.

Mary Lou was the first to speak. "Can you hear us?" she asked. There was no reply.

Andrea said, "Maybe they can hear us but can't speak."

Mary Lou said to the skunks, "If you can hear us, take one step forward." The skunks lined up in military fashion and took one step forward in unison.

"Good," Mary Lou said. "Now we'll ask questions. To answer 'yes' step forward; to answer 'no' step back. Which one is Matilda deMeow?" The skunk with the blond stripe and the twitching nose moved. "Ciesta Sands?" The fat skunk moved. "So you must be Octavia Rale." Mary Lou pointed to the pink-striped skunk, "and you, Prunella Peidmore." Octavia and Prunella lined up beside the others.

"I'm so pleased we've found you," Mary Lou said. "Now we must lead you back to the college. The faculty is meeting at 4:30 to set up search parties. If we hurry, we should be there before they leave."

Octavia lay down and panted. "You're tired?" Mary Lou asked. Octavia got up to step forward.

"They'll never make it back to the college by 4:30 if they walk," Julie said. "I wonder if they can ride on our propellants."

Octavia, who had just struggled to her feet, lay down again.

"No way," Andrea said. They stood looking at the skunks wondering what to do.

"I know," Mary Lou said. She walked round the clubhouse to where rows of golf carts were parked. Trying to look nonchalant she examined them looking for one with its keys in the lock. No; all were locked. Then she had an idea. Flexing her fingers she focused on the front cart and chanted:

For this golf cart to depart
I hex this cart to make it start.

The engine spluttered and then purred. Mary Lou quickly sat on the cart and steered it around to where Andrea, Julie, and the skunks waited. "Quick," she said. "Jump on before someone sees us."

"The cart will stink forever," Julie said. She was holding a tissue to her nose. She felt Matilda's beady eyes staring at her and she blushed.

Matilda, Ciesta, and Prunella were able to jump into the back of the cart. Octavia made a run at it but fell backwards. Feeling awkward about lifting up her old professor, Mary Lou helped her in.

"Now your hands will stink," Julie said.

"I can wash them." Mary Lou got into the driver's seat, and Julie and Andrea jumped in beside her after stacking the propellants in the golf clubs container.

"Water makes the stink worse," Julie said. "Don't come into our room like that."

"You can use hydrogen peroxide," Andrea said. "There's some in our lab. You mix it with baking soda."

"How do you know that?"

"Our dog got skunked once and that's how we got rid of the smell."

The golf cart trundled slowly down the driveway and onto the road towards the college.

22

The Faculty of Sophistry gathered once more in a lecture hall. The dean overheard someone saying, "I wish this damned business was over. I need to get on with some work." She felt much the same way herself. Their lives were too busy as it was, without the additional stress of disappearing faculty.

The dean walked on to the stage alone. Henrietta was sitting in the front row reading a *Journal of Speculative Thaumaturgy*.[9] "Where's Mary Lou?" the dean asked her.

"I expect she'll be here in a minute," Henrietta said without looking up.

"I'm not waiting for her," the dean said. Then added in an undertone, "As if this student hasn't caused enough trouble."

The dean called for silence. She reminded the faculty of the task in hand and then turned on the overhead projector to beam out a map of the area surrounding the campus on which she had drawn grid lines. "I have taken the liberty of dividing this map into areas, as you see. I propose that two faculty take an area to search."

She looked up to squint at the audience, then moved away from the projector so she could see them better. "Are there any questions or comments?" Silence. "Right. I suggest that you pair up, then each pair come up to the map and choose an area. I have paper copies of the maps too." She indicated a pile of paper. "I reckon it will take about two hours to search an area so we could meet back here after supper, at say…" she looked at her watch, "eight o'clock."

"What if we find them?" someone asked.

"I thought about that," the dean said. "If someone finds them, bring them here. Then Henrietta or I will propel around to find the rest of you and inform you of their return."

---

[9]   Published monthly by the Academy of Thaumaturgists

The first pair of faculty was on the stage looking at the map when the back door opened to admit Mary Lou followed by four skunks. "Here they are," Mary Lou shouted. "Our four professors."

The four skunks walked on to the stage and stood looking bewildered. At first the faculty was stunned, then as it recovered everyone began to clap and cheer.

"Well done, Mary Lou," the dean said. "Where did you find them?"

"At the golf course," Mary Lou said. "Three of us searched the forest. We ended up at the golf clubhouse. We were sitting having a drink when they appeared from under a hut."

"Can they talk?" the dean asked.

"Perhaps to each other," Mary Lou said, "but not to us. At least, we can't hear them. They can hear us though. They will step forward to answer 'yes' and back to answer 'no.' Matilda deMeow, would you step forward please." One skunk moved toward Mary Lou.

"Hello, Matilda," the dean said. "Nice to have you back with us, albeit in animal form." She wrinkled her nose. "We'll soon have you in human form again."

"Have you found the counter-aff?" Mary Lou asked.

"Not yet," the dean admitted, "but people are working on it."

After these words, Matilda became agitated. She ran to the door, looked over her shoulder, ran back, ran to the door again, and looked over her shoulder again.

"I think she wants us to follow her," Mary Lou said. The skunk took one step forward. "Yes, she does.

"Right," the dean said. "You come with me, Mary Lou, and you too, Henrietta. Okay Matilda, lead the way."

Mary Lou opened the door. Matilda ran out and stood in front of the elevator.

Henrietta whispered to the dean, "I'm not sure we should use the elevators. Someone is sure to complain about the skunk odour."

"Screw them," the dean said in a decidedly un-academic way.

"Do you want to go to your office?" Mary Lou asked the skunk. It stepped forward.

They took the elevator to the third floor and Matilda led them to her office. It was locked. The dean stared at the lock with her hand on her talisperson. The door opened.

Matilda rushed in and stood in front of a filing cabinet.

Mary Lou touched the top drawer. Matilda stepped back. She touched the second drawer and this time Matilda moved forward. She tried to open the drawer but it was locked. Matilda walked over to her desk and nosed at the middle drawer. The dean opened it and found a key for the filing cabinet. She riffled through the first files, stopping occasionally to read out the labels: 'Anthropoglots; Antefluvial expressions; Affarnishment; Afflatus – migratory; Archimages; Axonometry.'

"I wish you could tell me what I'm looking for," she said to Matilda. The skunk nosed at the drawer.

"I think she wants you to carry on," Mary Lou said.

The dean continued to search through the files. "Ah here! 'Aerostatic effluviosis'?" Matilda stepped back.

"I think they are in some sort of alphabetical order as everything you have read begins with an 'a.'" Mary Lou said. "So animopo-morphosis should be in that section." Matilda jumped forward. Each time she moved the aroma of skunk became more intense. Henrietta opened the window and leaned out.

"Ah here. Animopo-morphotic counter-affs." The skunk jumped up and down.

The dean sat at the desk and opened the file. "Here we are. There's a recipe for a counter-aff. Do we have these ingredients, Henrietta?"

Henrietta looked over her shoulder and read out:

3 hairs of black cat in heat
2 leaves of ranunculus picked at sunset
Saliva of a rabid bat
6.333 grams of Abraum Salts[10]
Egg of Chinese alligator
Pinch of shed skin of Bushmaster snake
1.239 pints of blood of Buffalo

Boil in lebes until slimy.
Concoct using a suitable chanting aff. Imbibe.

"I think we have most of them in the lab. Except for the Abraum Salts. That might be difficult." Matilda's tail drooped. "But not impossible," the dean said. "I can always call on another lab."

"We must make you all comfortable somewhere," the dean said in a soothing tone, "until Henrietta has concocted the counter-aff. Where would be a good place?"

"They need to be outside," Mary Lou said, "or at least in a room where they can get out easily."

---

10   Oxford English Dictionary. Mixed salts found above the pure rock salt at Stassfurt in Germany and also in the Isle of Wight, once thought useless, now used for producing chloride of potassium.

"I think the old Sorority Hall would do," the dean suggested. "Mary Lou will take you there and stand guard over you."

"I need Mary Lou in the lab," Henrietta said. "Could you find some graduate students to take care of them?"

"Yes," the dean said. "Or I will. No, I can't." She suddenly realised that now the four professors were found she could safely leave for the MAST meeting. Henrietta could be left to obtain the ingredients for the counter aff so she may as well go. And she would be back long before the deadline. "Let's go and join the others and I'll ask one of the faculty to look after them."

They returned to the lecture hall. The skunks were still on the stage but the faculty now occupied the seats at the back of the hall. They moved forward when the dean appeared.

"We have found the recipe for the counter-aff," the dean said. "Henrietta will gather the ingredients to make it. In the meantime, we will house the sk … the four faculty in the Sorority Hall. I need someone to look after them." She looked around. "Wanda, would you take on the task?"

"Certainly, dean," Wanda said. "What do they eat?"

"I expect they'd like some fruit and veggies," Mary Lou said. She refrained from mentioning worms, beetles, frogs and other delicacies that normal skunks enjoy.

Matilda moved forward and made a slurping noise.

"Oh, water. Of course," Wanda said. "Very well. I will escort you to the Sorority Hall and then find you refreshments."

"You come with me, Mary Lou." Henrietta picked up the counter-aff recipe.

"We'll be as quick as we can, dean," she added as they all left the lecture hall.

The dean returned to her office. Herman looked up with a wary expression but the dean seemed to have recovered from her anger over the fish. Nevertheless, he decided that this was not a good time to seek her views on radii and hemispheres.

"We have found the missing faculty. In the form of skunks. They are being housed in the Sorority Hall. Henrietta is working on the counter-aff." She began to gather papers into a briefcase. "As everything is under control, I'm going to MAST."

23

Once more Mary Lou found herself in the faculty lab. "Where's Marvin?" she asked Henrietta.

"We don't need a lirry to make up this recipe," Henrietta said. "It's a simple aff concoction."

"I'd like to see him anyway. He likes me."

"Oh, all right, I'll get it." Mary Lou paid close attention as Henrietta unlocked the door to the side room by keying in numbers. One, two, three, four, Mary Lou repeated to herself. Simple. Now I need to find out the code for the lab itself. Henrietta returned with lirry number WD40.

"Hello, Marvin," Mary Lou said delightedly. "It's nice to see you again." The lirry sent her a smell of orange blossom.

"That's funny. There's a note on its cage from Kinella saying that it won't perform," Henrietta said. "But it made a smell for you."

"Perhaps he's tired after yesterday?"

"Nonsense! They don't get tired so quickly." Henrietta peered into the cage. "It doesn't look sick, and it's been eating. I wonder what's wrong with it."

"Are you tired of living in a cage?" Mary Lou asked Marvin. She bent down to blow at him. In response he made a smell of roasted chestnuts.

"Don't put such ideas into its head," Henrietta said. "It probably won't perform because you have spoilt it." She turned the cage round so that the lirry could not see them. "Stop playing with it. We've got work to do."

"What would you like me to do?" Mary Lou asked.

Henrietta sat down. "We have a bigger problem than I made out in front of the dean. You see," she hesitated, "we do not have any Abraum salts. There's been no call for it as long as I've been here. I don't know where to get any either at this short notice. The main source is in Germany. Then there's the Isle of Wight. But both places are in a different time zone. And it will take days to courier it, if they do have it."

"Didn't you say we could try other labs? More local, I mean."

"Yes, we can do that." Henrietta sighed. "I shall have to call around, but I can't do that now." She looked at her watch. "It's nearly six o'clock and all the labs will be closed. We'll have to wait until morning. I'll have to get up at 4 a.m. to start phoning the labs in the east."

"Do we have everything else we need?" Mary Lou turned Marvin's cage round again and ran her fingers across the wires. She was rewarded with a smell of fresh baked bread.

"Yes I think so. Let's lay everything out ready," Henrietta said. "You count out the black cat's hairs while I measure the buffalo blood."

Mary Lou could not find the right jar after searching through several labelled as, for example, cod eyes, caterpillar fur, crow craw, cat meow. "Is it under b or c?" she asked Henrietta.

" 'b' I expect." Henrietta was busy pouring thick red fluid into a conical measuring cup.

Mary Lou searched the jars beginning with 'b'; bat pellets, brown toad, bird beak, blue blood. Although Sophists were able to sort things into alphabetical order by grouping the first letter together, they did not seem capable of using the second letter also. We went through this trying to find the recipe in Matilda's files, she thought.

At last she found a jar labelled 'black cat hair.' Using a pair of forceps, she carefully extracted three hairs, one at a time, and laid them on a small dish. Henrietta placed her measuring cup of buffalo blood beside it. "Right, what's next?" She picked up the recipe. "You find the ranunculus and I'll get the bat saliva."

Mary Lou started to root amongst the jars again. "It will be in a basket," Henrietta said.

Small baskets—some with lids, some without—were stacked untidily in a cupboard. "You need a spring clean in here," Mary Lou said to Henrietta.

"The lab assistant is off sick. He's the one who cleans up after us. Shhh a minute." Henrietta carefully dropped a few drops of viscous fluid from a pipette into a small glass container. "He foolishly got some spilt deer urine and ptomaine onto his hands and didn't wash them before he ate. His mouth looked like a pitted prune."

"Is he all right?" Mary Lou said with concern.

"He will be. We gave him an antidote of course, but he has to wait for his mouth to grow before he can return to work."

Mary Lou continued her search for the ranunculus and finally found a basket of dried leaves. She placed two of them on a small saucer. Meanwhile, Henrietta was pounding something in a mortar.

"What's that?" Mary Lou asked.

"Skin of bushmaster snake," Henrietta said over the noise of her thumping pestle.

"I've never heard of it." Mary Lou leaned on the bench to watch.

"The Latin name is Lachesis Muta but it is called 'suruccu' or 'bushmaster' in its native South America." Henrietta started to drone like she did in her lectures. "This reptile is the largest of the pit vipers. It may measure up to twelve feet and be as thick as a man's thigh. Its body, patterned with orange and black diamonds, ends in a rainbow-coloured head. Armed with fangs an inch or two long, its bite is deadly. It lives in…" At this point Marvin emitted a smell of sewer gas so strong that Henrietta was forced to stop talking as she gasped for breath.

After she recovered, she continued to pound the contents of the mortar in silence. When the snake skin was powdered to her satisfaction, she lined up the mortar with the other ingredients they had prepared. "That's all we can do for now. The egg of Chinese alligator is in the fridge and must stay there until we are ready to use it. If we bring it out now, it might hatch."

"Oh, by the way, can I have my ingredients back?" Mary Lou asked. If she did decide to go into business she better have the allspice anyway, in her possession. The other ingredients could be replaced, but there was obviously something special about the allspice.

"I don't see why not." Henrietta unlocked a cupboard and pointed inside. "There they are."

Mary Lou carefully packed the jar of allspice into her pack but left the other containers in the cupboard with a muttered, "I'll get those later." Then she said, "Can we go for dinner now?"

"Are you always hungry? Yes you may go. Come back here early in the morning.

I have to stay and feed the lirrys." Henrietta picked up Marvin's cage and headed for the side room.

"Can I come and help you?" Mary Lou said quickly.

"You're not supposed to enter the lab animal's room," Henrietta said. "But then, you're not supposed to be in the faculty lab either, and the dean said you could. So come on. I would like some help and then I can get on with my real work."

They entered a white-tiled room with a window at one end and three or four garbage pails under it. Rows of shelves lined each side of the room and cages of animals were stacked on them. The room smelled of disinfectant.

Despite the window and the white tiles, the room was gloomy, and it was a few moments before Mary Lou's eyes adjusted. Henrietta placed Marvin's cage on top of a similar cage, one that also held a lirry. Mary Lou moved down the row of cages saying hello to each lirry and blowing at them. Delightful odours of lilac and honeysuckle soon drowned the disinfectant.

"You certainly have a way with them, Mary Lou," Henrietta said. "Now, you can help me feed them then we'll do the mean mews."[11]

"Mean mews?" Mary Lou said.

"Yes. Look behind you."

On the other side of the room, small cages housed a different creature. Mary Lou walked across to examine one. It resembled a white mouse but with a solid body, more like a sugar mouse, and it seemed to be covered with eggshell instead of hair. A thin black stripe ran downwards from the top of its back to its belly so that it looked as though it were divided in half. A stump of a tail protruded from one end, and the other held a small head with tiny green eyes that gleamed at Mary Lou malevolently. It bared its teeth at her and she involuntarily backed away.

"That's why they're called mean mews," Henrietta said. "You have to wear gloves to handle them because they bite."

"What happened to its tail?" Mary Lou asked.

"We have to chop off their tails before they come here," Henrietta said.

"That's terrible!"

"No it isn't. Their tails go to infinity and they can't move until we cut them off."

"But why so short? Surely they could have a bit more."

"There's a critical point, two standard deviations from their means, their black lines, at which the tail continues to grow. Miss it and it has to be done again. Cutting tails off mean mews is a highly skilled job."

"No wonder they're mean if someone chops off their tails." Mary Lou moved closer to one cage and the mean mew hissed. "What are they used for?"

"Different affs," Henrietta said vaguely. She moved over to the garbage pails. "Now here is the meal for the lirrys. Put one of these scoops in each cage like this." She moved to the nearest lirry cage, opened a side door, pulled out a dish, filled it and put it back. "Then we'll change the water. I'll do the mean mews."

Mary Lou's mind was as busy as her hands. She wanted to rescue Marvin and keep him as a pet but she knew that if WD40 disappeared Henrietta would suspect her. All the lirrys looked alike as far as she could

---

11   The symbol μ (Greek: mu) is used to denote the arithmetic mean of an entire population. Or, for a random number that has a defined mean, μ is the *probabilistic mean* or expected value of the random number. If the set X is a collection of random numbers with probabilistic mean of μ, then for any individual sample, xi, from that collection, $\mu = E\{xi\}$ is the expected value of that sample.

tell, so all she had to do was change his label for another, less well known one. She quietly examined the cage labels as she put in the food. They were not in chronological order, and she even found WD982 even though there were only about thirty cages. The usual attendant was away, and who else would notice if one disappeared? She knew how to get in to the animal's room; now she needed to find out how to enter the lab.

When all the lirrys and mean mews were fed and watered, Henrietta and Mary Lou went back into the lab. "Thank you for your help," Henrietta said. "Now I can get on with my own work."

Mary Lou's plan was to exit with Henrietta and leave something behind. She could then ask Henrietta for the code to get in. However, Henrietta looked as though she was going to adjust her traffic light equipment so Mary Lou was forced to say, "Good night" and prepare to leave. But she still neglected to pick up her pack.

Mary Lou had her hand on the door knob when Henrietta said, "Wait a minute, I'll come with you. I must visit the skunks—um, the dissipated faculty."

They walked down three flights of stairs together and then Mary Lou stopped suddenly and said, "Phoney Philtres, I've left my pack in the lab." She looked at Henrietta with wide eyes. "Oh, I'm so sorry."

Henrietta frowned. "Can you do without it until tomorrow?"

"No, not really. It's got an assignment in it that's due tomorrow." Mary Lou paused. "You don't have to go back up. If you tell me how to get in I'll run up and join you back here."

"Alright, Mary Lou," Henrietta sighed, "It's four, three, two, one."

"I won't be a minute." Mary Lou ran upstairs, keyed in the numbers, grabbed her pack, and ran downstairs again to the waiting Henrietta. "Sorry about that," she said as she tried to conceal her delight.

24

In the Sorority Hall kitchen, Wanda was making a tossed salad for the skunks. She wondered what sort of dressing they would like, or if they ate dressing at all. How could she find out? Call out the available dressings and see who stepped forward? Finally, as the task of finding out their preference in salad dressing was more than she could face, she decided to leave the salad undressed. She wanted to get out of there as soon as possible; the smell was beginning to settle in her stomach.

Wanda dished out the salad into four bowls, placed them on a tray, and carried them into the main hall where the skunks were reclined on sofa cushions that had been placed on the floor. "Dinner," she called out as she set the bowls down in a row. She watched with satisfaction as the skunks gobbled hungrily. While they dined, she filled up their water bucket.

"I'm very interested in what it feels like to be a skunk. I want to design a questionnaire that I hope you will complete after you've reissipated. Would you be willing to do that?"

Of course there was no verbal reply; she hadn't expected one, but she was disappointed with no reaction at all. Slurps from the bowls indicated nothing but satisfaction. Then she had a thought. What if they never were reissipated? Would she be destined to care for them for the rest of their lives? No way; that was not why she'd gone into sophistry.

She took the empty plates to the kitchen to wash. "I'm going to my office now," she said on her return. "I'll come back later to see how you are. Now, you have water, you have shelter, you have beds, you have a place to hide. I will notify the security guard of your presence so there won't be any trouble from that quarter." She looked around and said, "Good night, I hope you are comfortable," before she left.

Ciesta was bored. She was accustomed to watching television in the evenings. "What do skunks do for fun?" she asked Matilda.

"How should I know? I've only been one as long as you have."

"We don't even have to forage for food… with Wanda fussing around… making us salads." Ciesta gave her back a good scratch.

"You would think some of the faculty would come and see us," Octavia said.

"We smell too much," Matilda said. "Henrietta did her best to hide her distaste, but I could see she had a hard time."

"It's funny that we can't smell ourselves," Prunella said.

"Can skunks smell anything at all?"

"Come to think of it, no. That's funny. Most mammals have a sense of smell," Matilda said, "and even with the highly developed sense of smell I obtained as a rabbit, I can't smell you three. Or even myself." She laughed. "But perhaps this perpetual twitch is affecting me."

"Well, it's certainly affecting me," Ciesta said as she paced up and down. "If you hadn't fudged the results of your rabbit experiment you wouldn't be like that."

"I did not fudge the results." Matilda spat out the words.

"I heard that …" Ciesta began.

"I could tell you a story," Octavia said quickly. "I'm very good at them."

"Go ahead," Matilda said.

Octavia settled on her cushion as best she could and began. "The Great Griselda was dean here many years ago, when I was a young Assistant Professor. GG we called her. Other names too, not all complimentary. She was very strict, and certainly no young woman of today would put up with her. But these were the days before Sophists' Liberation."

"How old are you?" Prunella interrupted. "I mean, how long ago was this?"

"Let's just say it was a few years ago," Octavia said. "It's refreshing for an old gal like me to reminisce. Where was I? Oh yes. The Great Griselda; she made many rules. For example, faculty had to wear their mortarboards with tassels to the front, not like now when we can choose which way our tassels fall. We had to record every aff we made, every ingredient we used, every effect—so tedious. One could spend more time on paperwork than on the job.

"Her rules for students would make everyone laugh today. Assignments were to be written in script using a calligraphy pen; typewriters were not allowed. Students had to wear skirts under their gowns, not pants, which made scooter riding even more difficult than propellants. Lebes had to be scoured daily with steel wool and soaked for four hours in Witch Hazel, even if they hadn't been used."

"What?" Prunella said. "That's ridiculous. We would spend half our time in the lab on lebes care and never get on to affs at all."

"That's right. That's exactly what everyone said at the time, but GG wouldn't listen," Octavia continued. "GG ruled the Admissions Committee with an iron fist. Her policies would not pass the Sophists' Rights Code today, they were so restrictive. For example, no student with other than black hair was to be admitted, and even if it was black, it couldn't be curly. Can you imagine?

"Well, one year, a young woman named Berninda sought admission. She grew up in a famous family of Sophists and thaumaturgists and was already well versed in our craft. She was completely suitable in every way, except for her flaming red hair. Not only was it red, it was curly. The Great Griselda refused to admit her. 'You shall rue this day,' Berninda said when she heard of the decision." Octavia squirmed on her pillow and began to pant.

"Octavia, although your story is fascinating, I am very much afraid that telling it will cost more energy than you possess," Matilda said. She wanted to be left alone to consider an idea that had been growing ever since she discovered she was a skunk; an idea for an experiment that would be sure to be funded; maybe even earn her a Chival prize. But she needed time to think, not listen to Octavia reminisce.

"Thank you for your concern, Matilda, but I am warming to my subject." Octavia's voice seemed stronger than usual and she continued. "After that, nothing seemed to go right in the school, especially in the lab. Affs had strange consequences or did not work at all; ingredients were mislabelled or had been substituted with something else. We had more explosions in a week than had formerly occurred in a year.

"A graduate student, performing a hex as part of her orals, was particularly affected. She was demonstrating the correlation between the length of hair of dog and the specific gravity of Zinchop's Brew[12] when her lebes' feet became those of a cloven-hoofed animal and it ran off. Brew slopped all over the grass boulevards and burned holes in them. Grass never grew again; instead, clumps of marijuana sprang up, much to the delight of students, but to the consternation of Administration. You can still see some clusters to this day, though gardeners are instructed to remove them regularly.

"After each incident, someone found a lock of red hair wound in a coil and pinned to a notice board or to a door. It didn't take long, of course, for people to realize that Berninda was behind all this. The faculty pleaded with Great Griselda to admit her but she would have none of it. She said

---

12 A concoction devised by Zinchop in 1592, used primarily as an additive to purgation affs.

she would teach this young upstart a lesson or two that would make her wish she had not messed with her school.

"Now as you know, part of our ethical code is that we don't put hexes on students, even when we think they deserve it, and that value held good in those days. But GG would not listen to the sane voices on faculty. She dismissed their concerns by saying that Berninda was not a student, and so the ethical code did not apply.

"No one knew where Berninda was, and hexes on people are easier if they are within earshot, eyeshot, or even noseshot, so you can measure their effects. GG was not deterred. She spent hours in the faculty lab concocting and experimenting, until one day, she called a faculty meeting to tell everyone what she had devised."

Octavia stretched before curling up again. "Go on," Prunella said, "What did she do?"

"She intended to alter Berninda's Gravity Quotient."

"Wow!" Prunella said, "That's pretty advanced stuff."

"Yes. Griselda was very clever. She was able to work out Berninda's GQ by analyzing her hair. She had to guess her weight of course, but that measure does not have to be exact."

"Can you remind me what GQs are?" Prunella asked. "I only read about them in grad school—we didn't have the right equipment to measure them."

"Each person has a GQ that allows them to walk on the earth. If it is altered upward, they float; altered downward, they can't lift their legs. Their Gravity Quotient Balance should be zero and it is held there by their Maximum Aerodynamic Ex-Factor, or Max Factor for short. This factor …"

"Hold on," Prunella said. "You're going too fast for me. Let me get this straight: I have a Gravity Quotient, which keeps me on the ground. The Balance of this quotient should be zero. If it's not, I would either fly or not be able to move."

"That's right," Octavia said. "Measurement and assessment of an individual's GQ is extremely advanced Sophistry and needs expensive, delicate equipment."

"Which we have in our school," Matilda said.

"Thanks to Griselda. It was her area of research and she had obtained a significant grant from the National Periaptic Society. Where was I? It's a bit complicated for me, but my understanding is that you need several measurements: weight, hair molybdenum in milligrams, and the Max Factor. The latter is crucial. To calculate it, there is an equation that must include phi.[13] It's a bit like pi.[14] As you know, pi*r^2 calculates the radius of a circle. I can't remember exactly what phi is, but it doesn't matter. I could explain better if I had a blackboard and chalk, but suffice it to say, it's a complicated formula. Once you have the formula for an individual, then you can alter it in the lab using some very specialized electronic equipment.

"Griselda was unable to quietly go to the lab to work on her experiment; oh no, she had to boast about it to the whole faculty. And that was her downfall. She had forgotten that those lecture halls can be viewed in the Bio-Hexonic Communications department by anyone who happens to pass by."

Octavia's voice became weak again and she stopped talking. When she seemed to have fallen asleep, Prunella gave her a nudge with her snout. "Go on, what happened?"

"Leave her alone," Matilda said. "I'll tell you what happened. Or rather, I'll tell you the rumours that went around, as no one really knows the truth. Before Griselda could find time to get to the lab, Berninda beat her to it. All we know is that as Griselda was giving a seminar, she left the ground. If someone hadn't opened the window, they could, perhaps, have contained her. As it was, she shot out and drifted away like those nannies in *Mary Poppins*. She was never seen again, though we did hear of a strange Sophist flying over Japan."

"Wow," Prunella said. "I've never heard all this before."

"Losing your dean like that is not something the school wishes to be generally known," Matilda said. "So keep quiet about it."

"How did Berninda do that—make Griselda take off, I mean?" Prunella asked.

Octavia stirred and said, "We think, but we don't know for sure, that Berninda had dyed her hair black and was around the place. No one except the Admissions Committee knew what she looked like so it would have been easy for her to mingle with the students."

"But how did she alter Griselda's Gravity Quotient?"

"Well, Griselda gave the formula away when she told us what she was going to do," Octavia said. "She couldn't resist showing off and she put the whole formula on the blackboard. Berninda must have been downstairs

---

13 Phi is the mathematical constant and an empirical (and therefore rational) real number, used to calculate a Maximum Aerodynamic Ex Factor. It is approximately 19/4.2.

14 Pi or π is the ratio of a circle's circumference to its diameter in Euclidean geometry, approximately 3.14159. Pi is a mathematical constant and a transcendental (and therefore irrational) real number, with many uses in mathematics, physics, and engineering.

watching her on the closed circuit television down there—the one that shows the lecture halls. We don't know how she got into the locked lab, but it is fairly easy to go through doors when you know how."

"But how could she have got hold of Griselda's hair?"

"You only need one and she probably got it from Griselda's velvet hat. Hairs tend to stick to velvet. And if she could get through doors, then she could get into Griselda's office any time," Matilda said. "What I don't understand is why Griselda flew away. I thought the formula just lifted a person off the ground so that they can't move."

"What happened to Berninda?" Prunella asked.

"No one knows," Octavia said. "We think she went to another college. She probably changed her name and the colour of her hair. Whatever she did she was a great loss to our school. Anyway, after Griselda took off, things went back to normal—or rather, they improved without her authoritarian ways, I am happy to say."

"What an amazing story!" Prunella said. "I'd love to meet Berninda. I wonder where she went?"

Octavia's gentle snores indicated she was asleep. "What shall we do now?" Prunella walked up and down restlessly. "I wonder where everyone is. We haven't had a visitor for ever."

As if in answer to her wish, Henrietta appeared. She stood in the doorway and indicated that the skunks should come outside; she could breathe better outdoors. They gathered round her on the grass.

"I came to give you an update on what is happening. Unfortunately, we have no Abraum Salts that we need in the counter-aff. As you may know, they are mixed salts found above the pure rock-salt at Stassfurt in Germany. They are also found in the Isle of Wight. Both those places are hours ahead of us, but I have left messages for them to call back. First thing in the morning I will phone North American universities but they, like us, may be out of stock." Henrietta turned away from the group to take in a deep breath of air. "There isn't much call for it these days."

The skunks groaned but Henrietta couldn't hear them. She just saw six bright black eyes and two pink ones staring unblinkingly at her.

25

Tired after her long ride, the dean reached the hotel where MAST was being held. She was still worrying about her dissipated faculty, but there was nothing she could do wherever she was. Except keep her hand on the rudder and maintain calm, perhaps—but surely the faculty could manage without her for thirty-six hours? The bustle of the hotel, the posters, and the air of excitement soon made her forget home and concentrate on the meeting. She had missed the opening reception but that was all; the business part of the meeting, the paper presentations and the symposia, had yet to begin. And she had a few hours to sleep before her presentation in the morning.

The speaker before her, a pompous thaumaturgist from Harvard, talked so fast that no one could understand him, and his slides whirled by before anyone could read them. Besides, his topic, *The Use of Alocacoc to Cause Frothing at the Mouth in Angry Subjects*, was not of general interest. Everyone knew that *F-essence* was effective for this purpose, so why look for something else?

The audience greeted the dean with relief. As raising the level of wrap-rage was the current hot topic, her study met with obvious interest. During the question period, several people lined up at the microphone and she answered them clearly and easily, except for one Sophist, who stood holding the mike as if about to croon and said, "What about paper?"

"Paper?" the dean said. "What about it?"

"I always wrap CDs in paper. Especially at Christmas."

The dean peered at the speaker. Had Octavia reissipated and somehow come to the conference? No; this person was quite young. But whatever her age, she clearly was not in possession of all her faculties. "The study did not consider paper," the dean said finally. "Paper is not likely to increase wrap rage, which was the purpose of the study."

"I thought it might bear some relation to my own study of the use of disintegrating paper plates. I compared those decorated with birthday designs to plain colours."

So that was it. This woman wasn't daft after all; she wanted to use the dean's time to promote her own study. The dean looked appealingly at the moderator but he was already raising his hand and saying, "That is not a question." He glared at the figure at the microphone, who moved away smirking. "Next question please."

After the session was over, during the coffee break, the dean spotted a tall, dignified thaumaturgist filling his cup. She edged her way towards him. "Dr. Kuroko. Circando, how good to see you."

He turned round and smiled. "Aurelia. I was hoping you would be here. Excellent paper you presented. Most interesting." He leaned forward and whispered, "I want to sound you out on a few things. I'm having a party in my room tonight. Can you come?"

"No. Sorry. The Select Committee on Periaptic Adornments is meeting over dinner. Besides, I hate parties at conventions. Everyone crowded into a small room—you have to stand up all the time—and the noise level! You can't have a decent conversation."

"Perhaps we could meet for lunch then? Today?"

They arranged a time and place, and the dean returned to the ballroom to hear more papers. She was particularly interested in one that had used a robot to collect tooth of crocodile. Clearly, robots would dominate the research of the next decade. They were useful not only in obtaining parts from vicious animals, but also in testing out dangerous affs.

She looked forward to her time with Circando. He had not only been dean of the co-educational school she attended as a graduate student, but also the supervisor of her thesis. She still sought his advice over her career moves, and now she wanted to know what he thought of her desire to sit on the Great Sophist Council, and how he thought she should go about securing a place on it.

They left the hotel to find a small, quiet café where they could talk undisturbed. As they had left behind any accoutrements of their calling and were dressed in plain black suits, they did not excite attention. At least, not the sort of excitement that usually surrounds magic art practitioners. Still, Circando's flamboyant white hair, piercing blue eyes, and long, white beard often caused people to stare in admiration.

"So," the dean said after they'd ordered their food. "What did you want to sound me out about?"

"Ahh, straight to business, eh?" Circando chuckled. "No room for the niceties."

"I thought we'd done those over coffee," the dean said. "I asked you how you are; you asked me how I am—what more do you want?"

"I'm glad to see you haven't changed," Circando said. "Right, well, let me see. First question: have you done any work lately on Gravity Quotients?"

"Not for a few years. Why?"

"I have a grad student, brilliant fellow, who wants to study them for his doctorate. He's having trouble putting a committee together. No one on our faculty has the expertise. Would you be willing to advise him? To sit on his committee?"

"I'm not up to date, Circando."

"Maybe not, but you understand the basic theories. It's just the equipment is more sophisticated, and you would soon learn that."

"Are you his supervisor?"

"Yes."

The dean thought for a while. "Okay, I'll do it," she said. "I'd like to catch up on the latest research, and there's nothing like a doctoral student's review of the literature to keep one up to date. And it might even get me going in the lab."

"You would only need to come down for his defence. We can communicate by the usual ways until then." Circando looked at Aurelia and nodded. "Good, good." He rubbed his hands and prepared to tackle the fish and chips that had been placed before him. He reached into a metal crate for the vinegar that nestled among an array of sauce bottles and liberally sprinkled his food. "What have you been up to lately?"

"I am taking a creative writing course," the dean said. "I want to write my memoir."

"Good, good. It's time someone enlightened the public about our art. I don't think most of them have any idea about the part we play in their lives." He chuckled. "They seem to think things happen by accident."

"Sometimes they do," the dean said, thinking about Mary Lou's brew.

"Ah yes. I always remember when you ended up with a four-winged bird that could only fly up or down and ..."

"Yes, well, enough of that," Aurelia said. "We all have our strengths and weaknesses."

They both chewed in silence for a few moments before Aurelia said, "Circando, I would like to be nominated for the Great Sophist Council."

"Hmm. Yes, it's time. You are ready." He picked up a chip with his long fingers and took a satisfied bite.

"Advise me. I don't know how to play the game. And usually I don't want to. But I do want to be on the Council."

"You're playing politics now," Circando said, "by talking to me."

"I suppose I am. Anyhow, you have to be invited to sit on the Council. How does one indicate one's interest?"

"I will have a word with the dean at U of Z if you like. I know her quite well. She sits on the Council and has some influence, I believe."

"Thank you, Circando. And I must talk to Adventitia—she knows everyone."

Adventitia Zade, dean of the hosting university's School of Sophistry, was difficult to find. The dean finally located her on a fire escape sneaking an illegal smoke. "Ha," the dean said, "caught in the act."

"Oh it's you, Aurelia." Adventitia pulled the hand she had quickly thrust behind her back up to her mouth and took a puff of her cigarette. "I hear you've lost four of your faculty."

"How on earth did you know that?" the dean asked.

"Word gets around." Adventitia stubbed out her cigarette. "I really must stop. The students call me 'the hag with the fag.' No," she continued, "Henrietta phoned me this morning looking for Abraum salts. I happen to know what they're for and Henrietta confessed, under my questioning. It's all right—I won't tell anyone."

"So-o, how do you know about Abraum salts?" the dean said.

"The same thing happened to us about five years ago. A student turned ten other students into cats," Adventitia said.

"That would be much more embarrassing."

"It was. We had to explain to parents why their darling offspring were chasing around campus meowing and screwing each other."

"Do you still have any Abraum salts?"

"I don't know. I haven't had time to look. I thought I'd go to the lab after the Select Committee dinner. Why don't you come with me? If we have some, you can take them back with you."

"That would be a huge relief. I'm sure Henrietta will find some. But we have to have the counter-aff made by, let me see, the day after tomorrow. If I can get the salts back tomorrow, the pressure will be off."

After dinner, the dean and Adventitia propelled to the university, to a new tower that seemed to the dean to be all windows. "New science block," Adventitia said when they reached the landing pad. "We managed to get a whole floor added, just for us. One of our faculty won a Chival prize."

"Huh," the dean grunted, "and there we are with small condemned buildings dotted all over campus. We're even in danger of losing those."

"How come?"

The dean explained the uncertainty of her school's future in the university, how none of her faculty were pulling in grants and now, if the administration found out about the loss of four faculty, it would spell curtains for the school. "They only need one excuse, and this will be it," she said. "They will say we're more trouble than we're worth."

"Stercus accidit,"[15] Adventitia said.

"Yes, but they don't realise that."

Even though the dean was at least a foot taller than Adventitia, she had trouble keeping up with the brisk pace of her small, energetic companion as they made for the faculty lab. 'Twinkle toes' was another of Adventitia's sobriquets.

"Why don't you approach Prance & Gambol for funding? They're interested in sophistry," Adventitia said.

"Aren't they a food corporation?"

"Yes, mainly. But they have several subsidiaries. I'll give you my contact."

When they arrived at the lab, the dean was filled with envy. 'Expansive' was the word that came to mind. And 'expensive.' Luxurious too perhaps—no: pretentious. No wonder they attract the best graduates, she thought bitterly as she said, "I'm not surprised that you're known for your research here. You must have the very latest of equipment. Why, what's this?" A stainless steel cylinder attached to rods and an electric meter covered with at least a dozen small dials, attracted her attention. "It looks like a Gravity Quotient servogadge."

"That's what it is," Adventitia said. "But no one here knows how to use it."

"The Spitzomate is missing." The dean twirled a few knobs and thought about the ancient enamel servogadge in her own lab.

"The what?" Adventitia looked up from the cupboard she was kneeling beside.

"The Spitzomate. Named after an Austrian thaumaturgist called Spitzo. It's the essential part that interprets the electrical readings."

"It's probably still in the box." Adventitia stood up. "I wonder where those Abraum salts are." She tapped thoughtfully on a bench. "Prance & Gambol donated that equipment when the lab was opened. Someone tried to put it together and then gave up. It's been sitting there ever since." She looked at the equipment and wrinkled her nose. "You can have it if it's any use to you. It's just taking up space here."

"What!" The dean rubbed her hands and then shook them in her delight. "Oh yes. Yes, yes, yes. It would be very useful. Very useful indeed. I've just agreed to advise one of Circando's grad students who's studying GQs. It was always an interest of mine, but I've let it lapse lately. But

---

15   Shit happens

this…" She stroked the cylinder. "This will revive it. Oh Adventitia, I can't tell you—"

"Yes, I can see," Adventitia said. "Now to get back to your dissipated faculty and the Abraum salts. That's why we're here."

"Where's the box?" the dean asked.

"What box?"

"The box for the servogadge."

Adventitia sighed and opened a store room door "It should be in here. Yes, there it is. And there, if I'm not mistaken, is the Abraum salts box. I wonder who put it in here." She clicked her tongue. "It belongs with the minerals."

The dean reached for the large cardboard box that Adventitia had pointed to and carefully laid it beside the servogadge. She held her breath; if the Spitzomate was missing then the rest of the equipment was useless. She opened the flaps, removed a sheet of Styrofoam and—yes, there it was, still in its sealed wrapper, its delicate prongs protected by foam sleeves. The device resembled an old-fashioned alarm clock with a bell on top, but with elongated thin legs that fitted into slots in the servogadge.

"Got any scissors?" the dean asked Adventitia as she struggled to tear off the protective plastic.

"What for?"

"To remove this Logos-damned wrap," the dean said, her voice rising.

"Ha," Adventitia said. "Aren't you the one trying to increase wrap-rage? Isn't that what your paper was about?" She sniggered. "How would you rate your rage right now on a scale from one to ten?"

The dean gave her a scornful look and continued to work on the plastic wrap with a fingernail.

"Oh for Logos sake, Aurelia," Adventitia said. She rubbed her talisperson.

Release the wrap on this Spitzomick
Before Aurelia sticks you with a pick.

Nothing happened. "It's not a Spitzomick," the dean said. "It's a Spitzomate."

Adventitia rubbed her talisperson again.

Release the wrap on this Spitzomate
Or Aurelia will make you levitate.

The plastic wrap fell away. "How's that?" Adventitia said with satisfaction. "Now before you start playing with this thing, I want to go home to bed. I'll get an assistant to pack it up tomorrow and ship it to you. Here's a bag of salts. It's small enough for you to carry." She stood between the dean and the equipment. "Aurelia," she said in a commanding voice. "Put it away. It's time to go."

26

Dean Virgo propelled home early Friday morning, the bag of Abraum salts tied firmly to her handlebars. She was riding her long-distance propellant, one with extra flanges, with panniers attached, and with a comfortable, sprung seat. These attachments made the propellant heavy, but she had initiated it with a particularly potent hex that gave it extra energy from the ionosphere. Only in gale force winds would the propellant be impotent, but she was unlikely to ride in those conditions anyway.

The meeting was not finished but the dean decided that, as she had delivered her paper and succeeded in her networking aims, the recovery of her faculty took priority. Now she had the salts and it was only Friday, with 24 hours to go before the deadline. She was confident that Henrietta would be able to make up the counter-aff so that the four faculty could be reissipated that very day.

She had let Henrietta know when she was returning with the salts, so she was not surprised to see her waiting when she landed on the faculty office pad. Perhaps it was because the prospect of a brand new servogadge excited her, or perhaps it was because the design of a study on the gravity quotients of newborns occupied her mind; whatever it was, she did not pay attention as she landed. Her heavy propellant crashed into the safety rail, tipped her into the arms of Henrietta, flew upwards on its own and landed on the sloping roof above them. With a slow kerthunk, kerthunk, it slid down the roof until it reached the gutter. The bag of Abraum salts slowed its progress by nestling into the gutter, leaving the propellant suspended from the roof.

"Oh, flaming faculty fossils!" the dean muttered.

"Are you all right, dean?" Henrietta said.

"I'm fine. I landed like a clumsy first-year student." The propellant, held by the bag of salts nestled in the gutter, jutted out over their heads. The dean reached up and pulled on the handlebars. Nothing happened. She pulled again.

"Perhaps we should remove the panniers," Henrietta suggested.

"I can't reach." The dean pulled on the handle again.

"I'll go and get a chair to stand on," Henrietta said.

While she was gone, the dean thumped her forehead with her fist and muttered several words that would have shocked Henrietta if she had heard them. Henrietta returned with a chair and held it while the dean climbed up. The panniers were in reach, and she was able to unbuckle them without a problem, but when she pulled on the handlebar again, the string holding the bag of salts broke with a snap. The propellant skittered down towards her, and the bag of salts, after hanging briefly over the gutter, hurtled to the ground.

The dean and Henrietta peered down at the bag. To the dean's horror, the bag had split and white salts were scattered over the concrete, with some joining a platoon of busy ants in its cracks. The dean knelt beside the pile with her head in her hands. "How much of this stuff do you need?" she asked Henrietta.

"6.333 grams."

"Thank Logos, Adventitia gave me more. A good scoopful in fact." The dean rubbed her talisperson. "Please let there be at least 6.333 grams of Abraum salts unspoilt. Please." She carefully lifted up the edges of the split bag to contain the salts lying on it. "Do you think it's worth trying to sweep up the rest, or will it be contaminated?"

"I don't know," Henrietta said. "I'll go and get a brush and sweep some up but I think we should keep it separate from what you've rescued. Logos knows what's in the rest now. But I think what you have will be all right."

The dean examined the pile that she gingerly held in her hand. "It doesn't look very much."

"Let's get it over to the lab and weigh it. I'll sweep up this first."

"I'll rescue my propellant and join you there in what, fifteen minutes?" the dean said. "Oh Henrietta, I'm so sorry. Just when success was in our grasp."

"Don't worry, dean. There are some salts on their way from Paraguay. They should be here tomorrow. Early."

"But we only have until 10:30 don't we? And how long does it take to concoct?"

"Everything else is ready. We only have one egg of Chinese alligator but I believe there's a spare in the student lab. I will check and order another if there isn't. They are easy to get." Henrietta hesitated. "There's something you should know."

"What?" the dean asked. The expression on Henrietta's face made her say, "Oh no. Now what?"

"The news of the skunks has leaked out."

"Oh holy Logos. How did that happen?"

"While Wanda was looking after the skunks, she notified security that they were there so there wouldn't be a problem. Of course, they wanted to know more. They don't know the skunks are faculty, which is a good thing. Wanda said they were part of someone's experiment. But it does seem strange. Head of security wants to see you."

Henrietta strode off. The dean left her propellant leaning against a wall until she had safely deposited the salts on her desk and then she returned for it and for her panniers. She was still wearing her travel cloak, which she removed and shook before entering the building again.

Henrietta had told Mary Lou to come to the faculty lab at 8 a.m., and Mary Lou was waiting there when she and the dean arrived.

"Have you got the Abraum salts, Dean Virgo?" Mary Lou asked.

"Yes," the dean said. "But I'm not sure there's enough. Could you get the scale, please?"

Mary Lou found the scale. The dean carefully tipped the salts onto the pan and stood back. Henrietta adjusted the weights. They all held their breath.

"6.332 grams."

"We're 0.001 grams short. Will that make a difference do you think?" the dean asked hopefully. She knew very well that aff and counter-aff weights had to be exact or the effect was usually lost.

Henrietta stood rubbing her chin. "Well," she said, "I can make up the counter-aff with what we've got and we can try it. If it doesn't work, we won't have lost anything, as I expect new salts tomorrow. We have all the other ingredients ready. Could you put them out, Mary Lou?"

Mary Lou opened the cupboard that the ingredients had been stored in and laid them out on a bench.

"Good. Now we just need the alligator egg and we're all set." Henrietta almost ran into the kitchen for the egg that she placed on the bench with the other ingredients.

"Can I see Marvin?" Mary Lou asked.

Henrietta stopped what she was doing. "It's been condemned."

"What do you mean?" Mary Lou said.

"Two professors tried to use it yesterday and it wouldn't perform so Kinella, who is in charge of lab animals, said it would have to be destroyed."

"Oh no," Mary Lou said. "No. You can't do that. Can I have him? I'll look after him."

"That won't be possible, Mary Lou. They are lab animals. Metamorphasised to be just that. We can't have them running around outside. Logos knows what would happen if they interbred with other species."

"But I could keep him in a cage, just like he is here. I wouldn't let him out, I promise."

"Mary Lou, right now, the most important task is to prepare the counter-aff so we can reissipate our faculty," the dean said. "Sit over there out of the way while Henrietta concocts."

Henrietta found a lebes and activated it with her talisperson. In no time, the water was boiling so vigorously that it spat out onto the floor. Henrietta waved her talisperson up and down, backwards and forwards to make a star-like pattern in the air before beginning to leap and chant.

Round my lebes with prancing feet
Throw in hairs of cat in heat.
Ranunculus damp from morning dew
Adds co-enzymes to the brew.
Saliva from a rabid bat
Would take the whiskers off a gnat.

Dual, dual, fire and fuel
Lebes boil to make this gruel.

Several grams of Abraum's salts
Will remove this student's faults.
Chinese alligator's egg.
Bison blood stored in a keg.
Dried skin of suruccu snake
For this counter-aff to make.

Dual, dual, fire and fuel
Lebes boil to make this gruel.

Henrietta continued to dance around the lebes and then added:

Although the Abraum salts are short
I hope that you will be a good sport.

Breathless from her activity, Henrietta sat on a stool to recover. If Mary Lou hadn't been feeling devastated by the thought of Marvin being destroyed, she would have been awed by the performance of an expert. To show interest she peered into the lebes. "Gross," she said. "It's all slimy, and it stinks of something gone bad in the fridge."

"That's how it's supposed to be," Henrietta said. "They can't possibly drink that. They'll throw up."

"Not if they want to return to normal." The dean picked up the lebes. "Thank you, Henrietta. Come on, let's take it to them."

Mary Lou, Henrietta, and the dean, carrying a lebes, made their way to the Sorority Hall. Wanda and the four skunks must have seen them coming, as they were waiting outside on the grass. "Is that the counter-aff?" Wanda asked.

"Yes." The dean carefully placed the lebes on a flat piece of ground. "But we're not sure it's exact." She turned to the skunks. "I think you should imbibe it one at a time. Wanda, do you have a bowl and a ladle?"

Wanda produced one of her salad bowls and Henrietta ladled some of the smelly, gelatinous mess from the lebes into it.

"I hope it's not too hot for them," Mary Lou said.

Henrietta stuck a finger into the bowl. "No, it's cooled down." She placed the bowl on the floor.

"Octavia, I think you should be first," the dean said.

The pink-striped skunk stepped forward to the bowl. It stood looking into it.

"Oh, get on with it," Prunella said.

Octavia turned round to look at her. "Have you smelt it? It's putrid, gross, totally disgusting."

"Octavia, if you don't want to try it, I'll go first," Matilda said.

The dean and the others could hear nothing of course but they were aware from the body language that the skunks were talking to each other.

Blowing out her chest as if gathering courage, Octavia stuck her head into the bowl and licked.

Nothing happened.

Not immediately.

But then, in the blink of an eye, the skunk was replaced by Octavia: pink hair, pink sunglasses, and all. There was a long silence before Octavia shouted, "Walpurgisnacht!" She hugged the dean, laughed, shook hands, and hugged Henrietta and Wanda and even Mary Lou.

"What a relief," the dean said.

"That was quite an experience," Octavia said. "One I would not wish to repeat."

"Welcome back," Henrietta said. "It's wonderful to see you."

"Right," the dean said. "Your turn, Matilda."

Without hesitation, the skunk with the long nose stepped forward and licked. Again there was a short wait and then Matilda appeared.

"Oh, thank you everyone. Thank you. It is so nice to be normal again." She shook hands with everyone.

"Very well. Your turn, Ciesta."

The fat skunk stepped forward and licked. Nothing happened. Several minutes passed and still nothing happened.

"Have another lick, Ciesta," the dean said.

The skunk licked again but remained a skunk.

"Oh for Logos sake," Prunella said. "I'm not waiting for this." She edged in beside Ciesta and licked at the slime.

After a few seconds, the young skunk disappeared and was replaced by Prunella. The fat skunk remained a skunk despite its desperate licking in the bowl.

"Why are you wearing a full professor's hat, Prunella?" The dean's voice was brusque.

Prunella reached up and removed the mortarboard with its gold tassel. Her face reddened. "How embarrassing! I tried it on while I was waiting for Octavia to return." She gave a nervous laugh. "Here Octavia, this belongs to you."

The dean bent down to peer at the remaining skunk. "Sorry, Ciesta, but this concoction doesn't seem to suit you. But don't worry, we will make another tomorrow. A stronger one. In the meantime, you must remain safely in the Sorority hall and Wanda will continue to look after you."

Wanda glared at the skunk but she just nodded and said, "Come on, Ciesta. Let's go in and make you comfortable." She entered the hall followed by a skunk waddling behind her with its tail drooping.

Henrietta whispered to the dean, "I guess the fraction difference in the weight of the Abraum salts was just too much for Ciesta's weight. I can't think of another reason why it wouldn't work, can you?"

"You must be right." To the others, the dean said, "Come on, let's go to the college. The faculty are waiting with coffee and then I would like to see each of you individually to hear about your experience and to find out what happened."

Suddenly Matilda let out a whoop of joy. "My nose has stopped twitching. Look at that." She peered first at the dean, then Octavia, then Henrietta. "Do you see a twitch?

No?" Matilda was clearly overjoyed. "Wouldn't it be wonderful if the twitch never came back and I have my beautiful nose again?" She fingered her nose. "Is it long and straight again?" She looked anxious until everyone nodded. "Oh, Mary Lou, I can't thank you enough. It was worth being a skunk to get my nose back." Surreptitiously she felt down her pants; the furry rabbit scut had also disappeared.

27

As the group of faculty made its way to the dean's office, Mary Lou hung back until they turned a corner and were out of sight. Then she pelted to her dorm. Julie was not in their room. She went to look for Andrea, who roomed next door. She was not in either, but as Mary Lou rushed out to try the lecture halls, she bumped into Andrea.

"Andrea. You've got to come and help me. They're going to kill Marvin—if they haven't already. I'm going to rescue him."

"Cool it, Mary Lou. I don't know what you're talking about."

"Marvin. You know. The lirrypoop I told you about. They're going to destroy him. Come on." Mary Lou started to pull Andrea in the direction of the labs.

"Okay. Okay. Slow down. Where are we going?"

"The faculty lab of course. Where the animals are kept. Come on. We may be too late." Mary Lou started to run.

After a moment's hesitation Andrea followed. "How are we going to get in?" she said.

"I know the number codes," Mary Lou said.

They ran up the stairs to the faculty lab. Mary Lou punched in 1-2-3-4 on the lock and tried the handle. The door wouldn't open. She shook the handle in exasperation.

"Mary Lou, chill," Andrea said. "What's the number?"

"One, two, three, four," Mary Lou said. "That's what I put in." She stopped for a moment, "No, that's not right. That's the key to the animal room. It's four, three, two, one." She pressed the numbered buttons in that order and the door opened.

"Wow," Andrea said. "Look at all this." She began to wander round the lab touching Petri dishes, jars of coloured fluids, and baskets of dried goods. She sniffed. "What's that funny smell?"

"You haven't got time to look around," Mary Lou said. "Come on. A prof. could come in at any moment. This is where the animals are." She keyed in the correct numbers and opened the door to the room with the cages.

"Gross," Andrea said as she walked in. Then "Phoney Philtres, is that a lirry? Aren't they cute?" She peered into one of the lirry cages. "Their eyes are like baby seals. Only blue." The creature made her a smell of liquorice. "Wow. Is that what you mean about them making smells? Aren't they sweet?"

Mary Lou hurriedly read the labels on the lirry's cages. "I can't find Marvin. Oh, where is he? I hope they haven't taken him already. Andrea, help me look. He's WD-40."

Andrea began to open the cages.

"What are you doing?" Mary Lou said. "You can't let them out. They don't know how to survive."

"I'm not walking out of here leaving animals in cages." Andrea continued to open the doors but the lirrys remained where they were.

"They're too high up. They'll fall," Mary Lou said.

Andrea lifted one of the open cages and put it on the floor. Cautiously the lirry stepped out and slowly looked around. She lifted down another. When the two lirrys saw each other, they moved together as if in an embrace, all the time emitting a strange, unidentifiable smell.

While Mary Lou ran up and down frantically looking for a label that read WD-40, Andrea lifted down all the cages until thirty lirrypoops circled each other on the floor. "I'll never know which one is Marvin now," Mary Lou said. "They all look alike."

Andrea moved to the other side of the room. "What on earth are these?"

"They're mews. Mean mews. Hey, don't let them out," Mary Lou said. But she was too late. Andrea had opened two cages and two mean mews ran out, down the leg of the shelving unit and across to the lirrys. With little squeaks and without hesitation they both attacked. "Stop," Mary Lou shouted but as Andrea didn't watch what was going on, she continued to move down the row opening cage doors and letting out a stream of mean mews.

"They're much better off free," Andrea said.

"Andrea, stop," Mary Lou shouted again. "They're attacking the lirrys."

The first two mean mews were biting the lirrys and removing mouthfuls of green moss from their bodies, exposing mauve flesh. At first the lirrys did nothing, then, as if under a command, they formed two rows. The front row squatted; the back row stood, like nineteenth century infantry, and faced the onslaught of the increasing number of mean mews.

Mary Lou sniffed as a strange smell filled the room. The mean mews stopped attacking and, with silly grins on their faces, began to gyrate. They ran in small circles, bumping into each other until, one by one, they lay on their backs with their paws in the air.

"What's that smell?" Andrea said.

"The lirrys are making it. I think it's nitrous oxide. Laughing gas. It's an anaesthetic. I had it once as a kid. Quick, let's get out of here before we're anaesthetised too." Mary Lou opened the door into the lab and ran over to open the window. There on the floor beside the garbage pail was a solitary cage with WD40 written on its label.

"Marvin," Mary Lou said. "Oh Marvin, I thought you'd gone." She peered into the cage. The lirry didn't respond. "Marvin, are you okay?" She poked a finger between the bars of the cage and stroked Marvin's moss. "Come on, Marvin. I'm going to look after you. You're mine now." Still the lirry made no response; he sat on his sawdust staring out blankly.

"Marvin, I want you," Mary Lou said. "Lots of us want you. You are *not* useless. You're wonderful and a great help." A faint scent of roses hit Mary Lou's nose and then a stronger scent and finally a full-blown odour of lilac.

"Oh Marvin," Mary Lou said. "That's better." She picked up the cage and turned round to see Andrea at the door with the lirrys formed up behind her in rows of two like a school crocodile.

"Come on, let's get out of here before the mean mews recover," Andrea said as she opened the lab door to allow the lirrys to leave. "Let's go down the fire exit stairs. Less chance of being seen."

The lirrys moved into the corridor and waited there for Andrea. As soon as she emerged they formed a neat line behind her. Mary Lou, clutching Marvin's cage, joined them and they headed down a side stairwell and out into a shrubbery.

"OK," Andrea said to the lirrys, "Scat. You can go now. Do whatever lirrys do when they are free." But the lirrys maintained formation, and every time Andrea moved, they followed.

"You look like the pied piper," Mary Lou said.

"What am I going to do?" Andrea moaned. "I can't walk round campus followed by these weird animals."

"You wanted to let them out," Mary Lou said. "I told you they can't survive."

They walked towards their dorm, Mary Lou swinging her cage and Andrea with a trail of lirrys behind her like a tail. No one saw them, as most students were in lectures. Once in Mary Lou's room, the lirrys came out of their formation and ran around, exploring. They seemed to be enjoying themselves, as they made delicious smells. Except for Marvin; he made the smell of vomit.

"Oh dear," Mary Lou said peering at him. "I've made him seasick by swinging his cage. Never mind, Marvin, you're settled now." Gradually the smell lessened.

"Why don't you let him out?" Andrea said.

"Because if he joins the others I'll never know which he is. They're clones, so they look alike." Mary Lou flopped on her bed. "What are we going to do now? I'm sure I'll be expelled for taking Marvin and for letting them all out."

"I guess I will too," Andrea said.

"Oh no," Mary Lou said. "It wasn't your fault."

"I let them out."

"Yes, but I broke into the lab."

The two students sat on the beds and stared at each other. Finally Mary Lou said, "I'm leaving and taking Marvin with me. I'll write a letter to the dean. You can pretend you found it and give it to her. Don't say you were in the lab. I'll say I let them out."

"But what do I do with all these lirrys? Every time I move their eyes follow me. They're like ducklings that have imprinted on me."

Mary Lou thought for a moment. "I'll write the letter now. Take it and say you found it in your room—leave the lirrys here. Pretend you've never seen them." She tore a page out of her notebook and wrote:

Dear Dean Virgo:

I've decided I don't want to be a Sophist. I want to be a Sauceress. So I am leaving to go to the School of Saucery in Saskatchewan. I'm taking Marvin with me. He was condemned anyway so you won't miss him. The other lirrys are in my room. I'm sorry I let them out. Also the mean mews. The lirrys zapped them with nitrous oxide.

Yours sincerely, Mary Lou

"There. Give this to the dean. And warn Julie not to come here until someone has collected the lirrys."

Andrea took the note. "You don't have to take the rap for me."

"I want to leave," Mary Lou said. "No point in both of us getting into trouble."

"How am I going to get out of here?" Every time Andrea moved the lirrys lined up ready to follow her.

"I'll stay here. You sneak out."

Andrea edged round the wall to the door then opened it a fraction and prepared to squeeze out. But she was not quick enough; two lirrys escaped with her. Outside, with two lirrys at her feet, Andrea attempted to open the door for them to return. Instead, more lirrys joined her. She went back into the room. "I can't get out without them following me. And I can't stand their big eyes looking at me like that. As if I've abandoned them or something."

"Is there something we can put across the door that you can climb over and they can't?" Mary Lou said.

They looked round the room. "We could put your desk across," Andrea suggested. They dumped Mary Lou's books on her bed and turned the desk on its side. While Andrea stood surrounded by the lirrys Mary Lou opened the door and slid the desk across.

"There," she said. "Hurdle over that."

Andrea scrambled over the desk and made off down the hall. The lirrys ran at the desk with increasing momentum and obvious despair. Their smell of blocked drains became so oppressive that Mary Lou stopped packing, grabbed one small bag, Marvin's cage, and her propellant and headed out, leaving the frantic lirrys behind.

28

The entire faculty of Sophistry gathered for coffee in their lounge to greet the three reissipated members. Octavia clearly enjoyed the attention. She sat like an enthroned queen surrounded by courtiers who listened, fascinated, to her tales of the encounter with the sheepdog, eating from a compost heap—she quite forgot her fight with Ciesta—and the perils of the forest.

Initially, one or two people expressed concern that the aff had not worked on Ciesta but then, as the others talked, they forgot about her.

When the excitement died down, the dean asked to see each of the three separately in her office, Matilda first.

"I am interested in your experience as a skunk, Matilda, but later. Maybe over a beer? Right now I want to congratulate you on your tutoring of Mary Lou. Even though her experiment had, shall we say, unfortunate results, she did very well, I thought. Do you think we should allow her to continue?"

Matilda sighed. "She did what we asked her to do. She made up a new aff. So we can hardly fail her on that score. And she has shown great initiative in recovering us."

"Uh huh." The dean nodded.

"The aff she made is quite miraculous," Matilda said. "We might be able to cash in on that."

"I never thought of that." The dean's mind became busy with the idea of using Mary Lou's brew to make money to save the school "Thank you, Matilda. That's a brilliant idea. Adventitia Zade told me her school gets grants from, now what was it—Prance and Gambol or something like that. I must get in touch with her."

"I doubt that Mary Lou will graduate. She's far too soft-hearted to be a Sophist. But I think we should let her continue."

"You're right. Especially if we want to use her aff. I shall let her know our decision as soon as I can. But we may have trouble with her refusal to use animal parts."

"Difficult indeed. But perhaps we could direct her to electronics. I know she's very junior for that but—well, I grew quite fond of her." Matilda stroked her quiescent nose. "She's quite smart, you know."

The dean asked Matilda to send in Prunella.

Prunella was nervous. She expected this interview, but she thought the dean would wait until they had recovered from their ordeal. She had her story rehearsed but she still startled when Matilda told her the dean wished to see her.

"How are you?" the dean asked, as the youngest of the four prior skunks entered.

"I've been feeling much better since we were found," Prunella said.

"No doubt." The dean leaned forward. "There are matters I wish to clear up before we lay this episode to rest. I would like to know how you transformed into a skunk."

"I've been wondering that myself," Prunella said. She laughed and avoided the dean's eyes. "I can only suppose that someone tampered with some fudge I'd bought as both Octavia and I ate a piece just before we dissipated."

"You took the fudge into Octavia's office, did you not?"

"Yes. I'd been to Grabville Market in the afternoon to buy it. I left it in my office while I copied the course objectives for Octavia. When I went to see her, I took a few pieces with me to have with tea."

"She was obviously the first to eat it. How come you ate some after you saw her disappear?" The dean waited for the answer to this all-important question.

"I didn't see her disappear," Prunella said firmly. She clasped her hands and held her two forefingers to her mouth.

The dean recalled, from a management course she once took, that touching the mouth during a conversation is a sign of lying. "Octavia said you were with her when she ate the fudge."

"I was there before she ate the fudge, yes. But not as she ate it." Prunella tried to keep her face straight. "I went back to my office to get an example of a student's historical research paper. That's one of the objectives for the new course. When I returned, Octavia was not there. I assumed she had gone to the bathroom."

"That's not what Octavia told me as we walked back here," the dean said.

"She must have forgotten." The success of Prunella's lie rested on Octavia's usual confusion about recent events. "Anyway, I was sitting there waiting for her to return when I ate a piece of fudge. Next thing I knew, I was in a lane with the others." Prunella laughed nervously. "I must say it has been a most unusual experience."

"I see."

"While I have the chance to talk to you alone, I want to tell you that I have been asked to apply for a position in a college, one where teaching skill is appreciated."

"And will you?" the dean said.

"Yes." Prunella lifted her chin. "I was head-hunted by a college in Ireland."

"I wish you every success, Prunella." The dean was glad that the Promotions Committee would be spared the job of turning down Prunella's application for tenure. "Now, please could you ask Octavia to come in."

Prunella left with relief. She told herself to remember to dispose of the jar of brew still hidden in her office before someone found it. She thanked her talisperson for her escape and shuddered at the thought that someone may have packed up her office thinking she would never return. They would have discovered the jar of brew and surmised that it was she who had doctored the fudge.

Once the feeling of relief was over, Prunella thought about the dean's ready acceptance of her proposed notice to leave. The dean hadn't even expressed regret at losing her best teacher, someone who had won a teaching award. Just showed what the university thought of teaching skill—nothing. They couldn't teach worth a damn themselves, nor did they appreciate someone who could.

Prunella hadn't been able to figure out how to get rid of the Promotions Committee and now they were all back, except for Ciesta. Ciesta was still a skunk; and alone in the Sorority Hall. But was it worth taking revenge on Ciesta? Not really. Besides, she had told the dean she was leaving, so getting rid of the Promotions Committee was no longer important. No, it was the dean she needed to exact her revenge on; the person who was so willing to allow her to leave, who did not appreciate a good thing when she had one. But how? That was the question: how?

Octavia wobbled in to see the dean. She was exhausted with the events of the last few days. My goodness, was it only just under a week ago that she was sipping tea in her office? How she longed for peace and rest.

"How are you, Octavia?" the dean asked her.

"I am worn out, dean." Octavia toppled into a chair. "I can't handle crises anymore; they never used to upset me like this. I remember when a student made my nose eight inches long. It was like that for a week. I wasn't the least put out. Then there was the time when my fingers shrunk to stubs. Now that was a trial." Octavia wriggled her hands uncomfortably. "I couldn't write or do very much at all. But I managed without becoming exhausted, as I am now."

"I won't keep you from your rest," the dean said, "but there is one matter I want to clear up. Prunella says she was not present when you ate the fudge. Is that right?"

Octavia frowned in concentration. "Well, I thought she was, but my memory is not what it used to be."

"She said she went back to her office to get an example of a student's research paper," the dean persisted.

Octavia pondered for a while with her eyes closed. The dean thought she had fallen asleep but then she said, "I'm sorry, dean, I just don't remember. She could well be right. We were talking about her objectives and one of them was to do with research, so she may have left."

"Well, don't worry about it," the dean said. "You go home and rest. Take as long as you like. I can cover for you."

The dean did not believe Prunella's story but, short of calling her a liar, there was nothing she could do. As Prunella had elected to apply to a college, she decided to leave the issue alone.

She was thinking that a session with her hookah might restore her when there was a knock at the door and Henrietta burst in. "Aurelia, there's been a disaster in the lab. All the lirrys have gone and the mean mews are all over the lab eating our ingredients and chewing on rubber caps and tubing. They've ruined my experiment on traffic lights—ruined it! All that work..." Henrietta strode up and down wringing her hands.

Before the dean could respond, her secretary rushed in. "Dean, the police are on the phone. They've arrested Herman!"

"Which police?" the dean said.

"Dean, we can't leave the mean mews to eat everything in the lab," Henrietta moaned.

"The city police," the secretary said.

Henrietta was about to speak again when the dean said, "Just a minute, Henrietta." She turned to the secretary. "What's he supposed to have done?"

"They didn't say," the secretary looked smug. He didn't like Herman. "They just said they have him in custody."

"Very well." The dean thought for a minute. "Phone them and tell them I'll be there as soon as I can." To Henrietta she said, "Right. Let's go."

As the dean and Henrietta hurried to the lab, Henrietta panted, "It must have been Mary Lou. She's been working with me. She knew how to get into the lab."

"She what?" The dean stopped in her tracks.

"Mary Lou knew how to get into the lab because I foolishly gave her the door code. She'd left her pack behind and rather than run back up all those stairs, I told her the numbers. Poor judgement on my part, I know."

The dean gave her a sideways glance and marched on.

"I know she wanted to rescue one condemned lirry." Henrietta continued. "But I didn't think she had it in her to be so destructive. And my experiment—I don't think I have the heart to start all over again."

They reached the lab. Henrietta punched in the numbers but before opening the door she said, "Be careful. They attack your shoes."

The dean held her talisperson and they entered the lab. She barely had time to take in the scene of devastation before an n^{16} of mean mews formed into a phalanx and approached with intent. Although small, the mean mews were as menacing as a herd of charging rhino with their bared teeth and gleaming green eyes. Without hesitation, the dean rubbed her talisperson and chanted:

You've been released by a Goody Two Shoes
Now into your cages, go, mean mews.
If you pause for one more chew
You will meet your Waterloo.

The mean mews turned tail and scurried into the animal room, up the bench legs, and into their cages. The dean and Henrietta followed and quickly secured all the cage doors.

"Well done, Aurelia," Henrietta said. "I didn't have the presence of mind to hex them when I came in."

"Ah, but you didn't expect them as I did," the dean said. "Now, let us assess the damage."

Henrietta examined her traffic light equipment. "They've chewed all the stop-cocks but…" She adjusted some glass tubing. "I may be able to rescue it after all."

"What else have they done?" The dean walked around the lab and picked up a few baskets. "They seem to have been into the dried goods mostly. I'll tell you what, Henrietta, I'll send the student lab technicians to help clean up. Then perhaps you could make an inventory." She looked into the animal room. All the mean mews were asleep. Empty lirry cages were piled up on the floor. "I wonder where the lirrys are," she said. "Surely

---

16   Statistical shorthand for "number." e.g. a random sample of n=500

Mary Lou wouldn't take them all. That is, if Mary Lou is responsible—and we don't know that."

"She's my prime suspect," Henrietta said.

"Could be the Animal Rights League. They're quite active on this campus."

"Hmm, I hadn't thought of that." Henrietta shook her head. "I trusted Mary Lou. I don't know how she got into the animal room; she must have watched me key in the numbers."

"We still don't know for sure that Mary Lou is responsible," the dean said. "Though it does seem likely. Anyway, time to move on. I must deal with Herman."

The dean strode across campus frowning. If Mary Lou was responsible for releasing the lab animals, she was turning out to be a royal pain. "She'll have to go," the dean muttered. "No question. I hate to expel a student, but this is too much. She's disposed of four faculty, created havoc in our lab—what next? No, that's it. That is *it*!" Then she had second thoughts: if the idea that had been forming ever since Adventitia talked about applying for a grant from Prance and Gambol came to fruition, she would need Mary Lou.

29

The dean found her propellant and set off for downtown. What, by all that flies by night, had Herman been up to? She should have supervised him better, but what with MAST and reissipating the faculty, she really hadn't had time. It will be that blasted jammer. He caused havoc on the first trial so Logos knows what he's done now.

She was soon to find out.

The city police station took up the first three floors of a high-rise on the main downtown street. Several blocks from it, every road was completely grid-locked with cars and buses. Traffic lights were out and people stood in impatient groups by their cars, but strangest of all, was the silence; no honking, no traffic noise, no sirens, until, as she neared the police station, she heard a helicopter. It hovered over an intersection clear of cars. Men dressed in ambulance uniforms were attaching a laden stretcher to cables hanging from the chopper. One gave a 'thumbs up' sign and the stretcher slowly ascended. At least he didn't affect those, the dean thought.

In the next block, the cathedral squatted in the shadow of tall buildings, surrounded by a welcome patch of green. No one was around so the dean quickly parked in the cathedral garden, removed her cloak, and left it and the propellant hidden behind a bush.

On the street, crowds of people blocked the sidewalks, and the only way to the police station was by navigating through the stalled traffic. When she finally reached it there was no way in; shouting, angry people blocked the entrance. The dean sized up the situation then used her talisperson and said quietly, "Anthropoids arreste." Like the child's game of 'statues' everyone froze in position. The dean wove her way through the immobile people to reach the front counter. A large policeman stood motionless behind it. He seemed to be staring at a small, white-haired elderly woman wearing a peaked, navy cap set at a jaunty angle. The dean squeezed behind the woman to be next in line. Then she carefully rubbed her talisperson again where no one could see, and said, "Anthropoids resume."

The officer rubbed his eyes. "You were saying, madam?"

"I'm here to report an incident," the older woman said.

"What sort of an incident, madam?" The officer appeared bored.

"At the mall."

"Oh, yes?"

"There were these two men sitting in my car," the old lady said.

"Doing what?"

"I just told you. Sitting." The old lady banged her purse on the counter.

"I think you better come inside and tell your story to another officer. As you can see we are really busy out here." He opened a door beside the counter and showed the woman in. Then he turned to the dean.

"I've come about Herman," she said. "I'm his boss."

"Oh yes. Come this way, madam." The officer opened the same door as before and let the dean into the front office. "Have a seat. Adams here will see to you as soon as he's finished with this lady."

The front office was full of chairs arranged behind small tables. Adams, a burly man with cropped hair and a bulbous nose, was sitting behind a table listening to the white-haired woman before him and making notes on a clipboard.

"There were these two men, big men, sitting in my car when I came out of the mall," the woman was saying.

"Doing what"? Adams said.

The woman raised her voice. "I just told you. *Sitting*. Is everyone here deaf?"

"So there were two men sitting in a car," Adams said in a monotone.

"Not just any car; my car."

"Did you know these men?" Adams's pencil paused.

"No. If I did, I wouldn't be here. Besides, they were big and one had tattoos all over him. I don't know people like that. It's a sad day when respectable people can't go shopping without being accosted."

The dean listened with interest. She pulled her notebook out of her pocket ready to record a story that might come in useful for her creative writing course.

"So, madam, you found your car at the mall with two men sitting in it. What did you do?" The pencil had begun to draw.

"I pulled out a gun and waved it at them."

"You did *what*?" A great black line travelled across the page.

"I just said. Do I have to repeat everything?"

Adams took a deep breath. "Where did you get a gun?"

The old woman looked at him coldly. "All women these days need a gun in their purse. If the police were more efficient we wouldn't need one. But you can't go to the mall these days without encountering crime. And now I find two men in my car just waiting to rob me."

"Where is this gun, madam?"

"Why, right here." The woman opened her purse and pulled out a gun and handed it to Adams.

"This is a toy gun," Adams said as he flicked the trigger. He handed it back.

"Yes, but they weren't to know that." She smiled smugly and put the toy gun in her purse. "They sure moved when they saw this. Leapt out of the car. And one of them was heavy—like a wrestler. But he had tiny feet. Have you noticed how many fat people have small feet?"

The dean wrote quickly and tried to hide her amusement. Adams managed to say, "What happened next?"

"When they were out of sight I unloaded my buggy into the trunk."

At this moment, the officer from the front desk opened the door and ushered in two large men. As soon as they entered, one pointed and said, "That's her." At the same time the older woman shouted, "That's them!" She began to fish in her purse. One of the men dived under a table. The other turn-tailed and ran out of the door.

Adams rubbed his mouth with his fist. "You better give me that gun." The old lady handed it over and the man came out from under the table.

"She's a nut case," he said. "She should be locked up. There we were just sitting in our car, waiting for a friend, and this basket case comes along waving a gun at us. What are you going to do about the dangerous old bat, that's what I want to know?"

"Keep calm, sir," Adams said. "It's a toy gun." He showed it to the man. "Did you say it was your car?"

"Yes. Well, Sid's car. But not her car for sure." He glared at the old woman.

Adams turned to the woman. "Did you think it was your car?"

"Yes, of course I did," she said. "Then when I put the key in the ignition that's when I realised it wasn't mine. I knew it was someone else's. Some poor innocent shopper who would come out to their car and find two men sitting in it like I did. So that's why I came here," she finished triumphantly. "To report the incident."

"Do you understand what trouble you've caused?" Adams asked. "I think you owe these gentlemen an apology."

The old lady glared at Adams. "Why? They look like robbers. They probably are for all I know. I was only protecting myself. The public are allowed to protect themselves aren't they?"

"Oh, forget it," the man said. "Get her put away. Come on, Sid." He joined his friend who was standing in the doorway and they left.

"Typical," the old lady said as she picked up her purse. "Give me my gun."

"No. I'm holding it as evidence," Adams told her.

"I'll get another one." The elderly woman moved her cap to the back of her head and lifted her nose.

"You do that, madam" Adams stood up and opened the door for her.

"I can tell you, I am not happy with the way I've been treated. But that's what you expect from the police these days. It is not safe to walk around any more and I shall let the chief…" The voice faded as the woman left.

All this time the dean had been recording the scene with amused interest. It merely confirmed her views about the idiotic behaviour of humans, but she might get a good short story out of it. When Adams came over to her, her thin lips were curved and her eyes gleamed. "You're here about Herman, I understand?"

The dean nodded. "We're holding him as a possible case of diminished responsibility," Adams said. "I understand you're in charge of him?"

The dean nodded again. Adams led her down a corridor and into a small room bare of furniture except for a table and four chairs placed beneath a barred window. Herman was sitting on one of the chairs. The jammer lay on the table. He stood up when the dean came in and gave her his goofy smile.

"This man said he stopped the traffic with that thing," the officer said without preamble.

"And you believed him?" the dean said. She stared at Adams in disbelief.

"Well." Adams hesitated. "Something stopped the traffic. And not only that, but two pace-makers as well. Those people could have died."

That explains the helicopter and the ambulance, the dean thought. She turned to face the officer with her back to Herman. She rolled her eyes, grimaced, and whispered, "He's a bit simple. You can see that. How could his toy possibly stop traffic?"

"That's what I told my boss," the officer whispered back. "But he wanted to make sure." He turned to Herman. "I've asked Herman here to give me a demo, and he said he would when you got here."

"Yes, I want to show them how my jammer works," Herman said. "It's wonderful. You should see what it can do."

Oh Logos help me, thought the dean. How can I un-aff the thing while the officer's here? She thought quickly before handling her talisperson and saying, "Anthropoids arreste."

The officer froze but not Herman. The dean was amazed that the term 'anthropoid' didn't cover him. It means he's a warlock, she realized with a shock. Why didn't she find that out before? Her mind was abuzz but she didn't have time to think about it until she had got Herman out of the police station.

"What are you doing?" Herman said. "I can't just walk out. They'll come and arrest me."

"I'm not here to rescue you. I'm here to make sure this damn jammer does no more harm."

"No. Please," Herman said. "I've just got it working. And I want to show them what it can do."

"If it's working, then turn everything on again," the dean ordered.

Herman shuffled his feet. "Well, it turns things off but I haven't figured out how to turn things on again. But I can still show them how it works."

"Don't be ridiculous, Herman. Have you seen the havoc you've caused? You'll be jailed for the rest of your life. Shush. I've only got three minutes before the arreste hex wears off." She held her talisperson over the jammer and began to say, "Shall I compare you to a toy remote," when Herman grabbed it and held it to his chest saying, "No, no, please."

The dean continued by waving her talisperson over him.

You are less potent and less splendid.
Panda, roebuck, Billy goat
Herman's jammer! Your power's suspended.

She hoped there were enough environcouls to support the aff but there was nothing else she could do.

When the officer came to life, Herman was hugging his jammer, tears rolling down his cheeks.

"He thinks you're going to take it away from him," the dean said.

"No, Herman," Adams said. "I just want you to show me how it works. You said it switches off engines, right? So we need to find an engine but all those round here are off all ready." He thought for a moment. "Come into the kitchen. There's a microwave oven. You can try it on that."

Herman's, "No, it won't work on that," was drowned out by the dean's loud, "That would be perfect," as they followed the policeman into the staff kitchen.

The room was empty. The officer placed a cup of water in the microwave and turned it on. "Okay, Herman. Go for it."

Herman paced ten steps from the oven, adjusted dials on the jammer and pressed 'Start.' The oven continued to hum.

The officer rolled his eyes at the dean. "Give it another try, Herman," he said.

Herman fiddled with his dials again. Still the microwave continued.

"Right," the officer said. "I think we've wasted enough time on this. You're free to go."

Outside the police station, the crowd had thinned a little. "How did you get here, Herman?" the dean asked.

"By bus," he said.

"Well seeing you've managed to stop them all, you'll have to walk. I'll see you back on campus." The dean strode off in a decidedly bad mood, to retrieve her cloak and propellant and return to her office.

On the way, she thought about her guess that Herman was a warlock. If he was, then she must ensure that he receive proper training. Underused or bored warlocks could be a menace. They insisted on experimenting all the time and, if they were untrained, they could cause havoc and give Sophistry a bad name. If she hadn't rescued him from her previous university, Logos knows what trouble he would have caused. At least she had kept him busy. And now, with his amazing heritage, he could prove invaluable. She vowed to consult Circando Kuroko to find out how to prove his warlockship and then locate a proper school for him. As a bona fide warlock there should be no problem in finding him a place in a good university. In fact, she might even get him a scholarship.

When the dean reached her office, her secretary told her that a student had delivered a note from Mary Lou. The dean read that Mary Lou was leaving to become a sauceress. "What's Mary Lou's room number? And who's her roommate?" she asked.

Once again she marched across campus, this time to the student dorm, to Mary Lou's room. A sauceress indeed. Well, she should make a better sauceress than a Sophist. But she can't leave now; not unless we can make her brew without her. Since Adventitia had suggested applying to Prance and Gambol, or whatever the corporation calls itself, the idea of approaching them with the wonders of Mary Lou's brew had taken root. As they were a major food corporation, they might be interested—very interested. Until she could follow up on the idea, Mary Lou had become an asset rather than a liability. Now the question of keeping her was more important than expelling her. Whatever happens, the dean vowed, we must not allow her to leave,.

The lirrys lay in a heap in the middle of Mary Lou's room, their snores punctuated with small grunts. The dean climbed over the desk that blocked the doorway and stood looking down on them. They didn't move. You look pooped, she thought. A faint odour of garlic reached her. She pushed a pile of books out of the way and sat on the bed. How was she to get the lirrys back to the lab? Would they be able to balance on a propellant so she could transmit them back? No, there were at least thirty of them – a significant mass. A wheelbarrow; where could she get a wheelbarrow? No, nothing for it, they would have to walk. But what a public spectacle she would make; a dean followed by a bevy—was that the right word? What was the collective term for lirrypoops? A gaggle? No, a chuckle, that was it; a chuckle of lirrypoops.

Apart from the embarrassment, there was the question of secrecy. It was not generally known that Sophists used animals in their experiments, nor that the animals had been metamorphasised for the purpose. Although it was accepted by the university that animals such as rabbits and mice were used for experiments in physiology, for example, she knew Sophistry would be censured for doing the same, even though the animals had been bred for the purpose. No, crossing campus with them on foot was asking for trouble. The school would be picketed by Animal Rights activists, they would have their lab invaded, students would be ostracized—clearly some other solution had to be found.

The dean heard a noise in the corridor. Students must be returning from lectures. She hurriedly pushed the desk to one side and closed the door. Then she hexed the door so that no one but herself could enter. Safe from intrusion, she returned to the problem of transporting the lirrypoops. She could change them into other creatures, ones that would follow her and that wouldn't arouse comment. Dogs, for example. However, animo-transformation affs were not her strong suit. In fact, they always ended in disaster. After the four-winged bird episode, Circando had advised her to concentrate on other forms of Sophistry.

She needed help. Leaving the lirrypoops to sleep, she headed for the lab to see if Henrietta was still there.

The faculty lab was almost back to its normal untidy, though functional, self when the dean arrived. "Not too much damage, dean, I'm happy to report," Henrietta said, "And I've got my experiment going again." She happily indicated the flask of bubbling purple liquid.

"I've found the lirrypoops," the dean said. "They're in Mary Lou's room. They've pooped over everything but she's not here to clean up. She's left to become a sauceress."

"Good choice," Henrietta said.

"Not any more," the dean said. "We may need her and her brew to save the school." She explained her idea of applying to an industry for a grant.

"Why, dean, that's a great idea. Do you think they'd be interested?"

"They've supported Adventitia. With a lab to die for. And equipment. They would surely be interested in a taste enhancer? But later. The immediate problem is how to get the lirrys back here."

"Walk them back. They're very military, you know. They will form ranks and march. Not that we ask it of them, but that is one of their features."

"I do not wish to march across campus followed by a chuckle of lirrypoops," the dean said. "I would like to uphold some of the dignity of my office."

"I see." Henrietta stopped fiddling with her equipment to concentrate on the dean.

"Do you have some sort of conveyance?" the dean asked. "A wheelbarrow, for example?"

"There's this trolley." Henrietta pointed to the two-shelved cart that she had used for Mary Lou's equipment. "We could pile their cages on it."

"It would take several journeys," the dean said. "There must be an easier way."

"Hmm," Henrietta grunted. She strode up and down rubbing her hands. Finally she nodded. "I know. Get your propellant and meet me in Mary Lou's room."

30

Prunella toyed with the idea of using the brew on the dean, but decided it was too risky now that everyone knew its effect. So, not knowing that Mary Lou's brew had lost its dissipation properties and now caused delicious mouth sensations, she flushed the contents of her hidden jar down the toilet and returned the washed jar to the store room.

The dean had given the three dissipated faculty several days off to recover but Prunella, on the pretext that she had a submission deadline for *Sophistry Pedagogy*, hung around the faculty offices and lounge. She was looking for an opportunity for revenge—if not on the dean in person, then on the school.

The dean had asked her to write a report about her experience as a skunk. It was as Prunella was composing her thoughts for the report that she remembered Octavia's story about altering Gravity Quotients. If she could make this dean drift away like the Great Griselda...

The *Encyclopaedia Mysteriatica* had little to say about Gravity Quotients other than a definition, and most of Prunella's other texts were on education. She normally avoided the library; it was full of books written by dodos, but now she eagerly visited it. To her surprise, there were several shelves of texts devoted to GQs. She pulled out *Gravity Quotients Explained* and took it to a table.

Pages and pages covered with formulae and diagrams baffled her. She flicked through them quickly as she realised that, without intense study, all this was beyond her. What she wanted was a simple 'How To' book: how to calculate the individual formula, how to put the equipment together, and how to manipulate the hair; in other words, a form of Coles Notes. But she knew she would never find such simplicity in a university library. Perhaps the Institute of Technology would supply more practical texts, but they did not have a School of Sophistry, so they would not house the appropriate manuals. Maybe someone had written *Gravity Quotients for Dummies*? There were Dummy books for everything else, so why not that?

Stumped, Prunella sat at the table doodling on her notebook. Was there anyone who could show her what to do? If only she could find Berninda. But Octavia had said the incident occurred years ago and no one knew what had happened to her. She wondered if any of the older faculty knew how to use the equipment. Henrietta perhaps, or Matilda? She would find out.

Then there was the problem of the hair. Matilda had said only one was needed but one was as difficult to acquire as several. If Prunella could get hold of the dean's hat she would find a hair there. Or maybe on the shoulders of her velvet ceremonial gown. The task was to visit the dean's office when neither she nor the secretary was around. But then the office would be locked, and Prunella had never mastered the art of opening locked doors. Could she get in while the secretary was there and not the dean or Herman? On the pretext of delivering something perhaps? But the secretary would accept delivery and think it strange if Prunella insisted on entering the office. In her frustration, Prunella scratched her pen so hard that the paper tore.

The dean and Henrietta arrived at Mary Lou's room to find Julie and three or four students trying various keys in the lock. Julie's mouth dropped open when she saw Dean Virgo, an infrequent visitor to the dorms. "I'm not trying to break in," she said. "This is my room but my key won't work."

"I'll handle this now," the dean said to the other students. "You may go to your rooms." When they were out of earshot she said to Julie, "It won't open because I have put a hex on it for reasons I will explain later." She was about to say that the room was full of lirrypoops but she wanted to watch Julie's reaction when she saw them. The dean suspected that Mary Lou had not been alone in the lab and if Julie was not surprised at the sight of the lirrys, then she would know that Julie was involved somehow.

The dean used her talisperson to undo the hex and Julie opened the door with her key. The lirrys were running around the room and scampered to greet her. "Phoney Philtres, what are those?" Julie's amazement was genuine and the dean knew that she was not implicated.

"They are lirrypoops—lab animals. Mary Lou let them out and brought them here. I'm afraid they've made a bit of a mess. The lab assistant is away or I'd send him over to help you clean up."

"Urgh." Julie lifted up her foot to examine the sole of her shoe. She looked around the room. "They've crapped everywhere."

"Yes, I'm sorry about that. Henrietta and I are about to remove them." The dean turned to Henrietta. "Over to you. How do you propose to get them out of here?"

"They are going to transmit with us," Henrietta said. "Are you ready?" She pointed her talisperson at the lirrys and chanted:

Now it's time to fly the coop
So sprout two wings each lirrypoop.
As we have no taxicab
Fly with us to the faculty lab.

The lirrypoops were strange-looking creatures at the best of times, but with green bat wings that emerged close to their heads and attached to their front paws, they were comical in their freakishness.

"Are they going to be able to fly with those?" The dean sounded doubtful.

"We'll soon find out," Henrietta said. "Come on; let's lead them to the lab." She opened the door and marched purposefully out. The lirrys remained motionless. Julie, clearly anxious to get rid of them, flapped her gown behind them until they formed a column and followed Henrietta.

The dean said, "Julie: you are to tell no one, I mean no one, about the lirrypoops. As a reward I will allow you to work with one. Make an appointment to set that up." She hurried off to form a rear guard.

Henrietta started her propellant and hovered, waiting for the lirrypoops, who clustered uncertainly near the launching pad and made no effort to leave it. "You'd better launch, dean," Henrietta shouted. "The aff said they were to follow us, not just me."

The dean levitated her propellant and hovered with Henrietta. They both wafted away slowly as the lirrys became more and more agitated at their departure. When they were about twenty feet from the pad, the lirrys finally flapped their wings, formed pairs, and followed the leaders.

They were able to fly—upside down with their legs in the air. These they kicked as if to give them extra momentum. The dean glanced behind her and thought that if anyone saw her and Henrietta on propellants, followed by a stream of green-winged, inverse creatures, she could forget all about dignity. But most people were at dinner, so they reached the lab without detection.

Once in the lab, the lirrys seemed unable to turn upright. They landed on their backs with their wings extended and their feet pointing in the air.

"Oh for Logos sake," Henrietta said. She chanted again:

Now it's time to return to your cages
Even though you've been gone for ages.

So off with the wings and in with the food
And back you go into laboratory mood.

The lirrys returned to their usual form and stood up. In formation they followed Henrietta into the animal room and scampered towards their cages. The dean helped Henrietta stack the cages and fill them with food and water. Then she said, "I need a drink. Badly. Let's go to the Faculty Club."

Matilda was seated in their favourite corner of the Faculty Club lounge when they walked in. Judging by the array of dirty glasses before her, she had been there for some time.

"I thought you were at home recovering from your skunk experience," the dean said, as she put down her gin and tonic and a bowl of nuts.

"I waj," Matilda said. "But I can recover jush as well here. Cheers." She reached for her glass. "Here's to UBC and all who shail in her."

The dean's lips twitched. Matilda had always struck her as prim and staid, two qualities she didn't care for. She liked assertive people; people who said what they thought and were willing to take a stand. She had often wanted to shake Matilda out of her demureness. Now, since becoming a skunk, Matilda had an air of authority and, how would she put it, a ribald posture? No, not ribald, a word associated with drunks in taverns. A more playful word—jocular perhaps. "Cheers," she responded, and raised her glass.

Henrietta lay back with her eyes closed and her mouth set in a firm line.

"We've had a diabolical time," the dean said, and proceeded to tell Matilda about the escape of the lirrypoops and mean mews. She wanted to sound off about Herman too but that would have led to explanations she didn't want to make. "Now Mary Lou has gone off to become a sauceress," she added.

"Besht wishes to her." Matilda raised her glass and drained it.

Henrietta opened her eyes and sat up. "We haven't heard about MAST yet, dean. How did it go?"

"I think my paper was well received. And I met some old colleagues. But the best thing is—I've been given a brand new servogadge." The dean clapped her hands in delight.

"Besht wishes to you too, dean." Matilda raised her hand to order another drink.

"Thank you," the dean said.

"How did you get hold of a servogadge?" Henrietta said. "I thought they're outrageously expensive."

"They are. But Adventitia's school is well-endowed; so well, in fact, that Prance & Gambol donated a servogadge that no one there knows how to use. So she gave it to me," the dean said.

"Do you know how to use it?" Henrietta asked.

"I used to. Gravity Quotients were an interest of mine at one time. And now I've been asked to sit on a doctoral student's committee and his subject is GQs."

"Funny you should menshon Gravity Quotients," Matilda said. "Never hear of them normally. Never come up. And now they've come up twice in a matter of daysh."

"Really?" the dean said.

"Yesh. Octavia told us a story about an old dean, Grishelda, I think the name was. Sounded like a tyrant. A bitch of a witch, in fact." Matilda began to shake with mirth until tears ran down her face. "A bitch of a witch. Neat, eh?" She lay back in her chair cackling with laughter and hugging her knees.

Henrietta's face was set but the dean could barely contain her amusement. Go for it, Matilda, she thought. She was about to speak when Matilda sat up and seemed to pull herself together to continue her story. "Yes, this Grishelda dean wouldn't let a student in because she had red curly hair. Imagine that. So the student started playing tricks. So-o-o, Grishelda planned to mess with her Gravity Quotient, only the student beat her to it and made her fly away. Flew right out. During a seminar."

Matilda drained her glass and raised her hand again. "What I don't undershstand..." She hiccupped. "What I don't undershstand is why she flew away. Don't undershstand it at all. I thought altering a GQ simply makes people leave the ground and hover. Don't undershstand why she flew off."

"You use the reciprocal of phi in the formula instead of phi," the dean said.

Matilda and Henrietta stared at her. "I studied them in graduate school," the dean said. "That's why I'm keen to get back into that field. By the way, Henrietta, will you let me know when the servogadge arrives? I want to unpack it myself."

"Wouldn't you say that the recovery of Ciesta takes priority?" Henrietta said.

"Of course, of course. I hadn't forgotten about her, believe me," the dean said. "I shall be in the lab first thing in the morning to help you, Henrietta."

After Wanda had made a salad and said, "Goodnight," Ciesta found herself alone in the Sorority Hall. She wanted to express her disappointment about being the only one who did not reissipate, but Wanda, of course, could not hear her lamentations. Now, alone in the small sitting room off the main hall, she stomped around in a circle shouting, "Bugger and damn and a pound of ham," until she began to feel better.

The rhythm of her clomping and of her chant left her energized and wanting action. She certainly did not feel like relaxing on the cushions Wanda had laid out for her. She poked her nose through the slightly open door and then pushed so she could wander into the main hall. Ciesta remembered it as quite small but now it seemed like a cathedral. Windows lined both sides of grey-painted wooden walls giving enough light for her to look around. Beneath the windows, stacks of folding chairs meant that the floor space was empty and ready for dancing. Sounds of ABBA's *Super Trouper* came faintly from somewhere on campus.

In her imagination, Ciesta danced as if in a chorus line, lifting her legs, shaking her hips and whirling her arms to the rhythm of the music. In reality, she was a cumbersome, ungainly animal gyrating unsteadily in the middle of the hall. And this was the sight that met the eyes of the young couple who had crept into the hall and switched on the light.

"What the heck?" said the young man.

"Be careful, Mike. It might have rabies," the young woman said. She was backing away but Mike, bent down peering, shuffled towards Ciesta.

Ciesta stopped dancing. What had Matilda done when she met the sheepdog? She stomped her front feet.

"Mike, come back here," the young woman shouted. "It's going to spray."

But Mike continued to inch forward.

Let's do it, thought Ciesta. With stiff legs she strutted towards the young man. He stopped but didn't back away. When she was about four feet away, she turned her back on him. Now what? She bore down as though to have a bowel movement and a satisfying jet of oil streamed down Mike's jeans. While he inspected the damage, Ciesta made a run for the sitting room.

"That's it, Mike," the young woman said. "You're on your own."

"I'm going to fix that skunk," Mike said and headed for the sitting room.

"No, you're not," the woman said. "Come out of here or I'll go for security."

Mike picked up an old hockey stick from a corner of the hall and, with a venomous look on his face, threw open the door of the sitting room. He groped for a light switch but couldn't find one. When his eyes adjusted to the dim light from the window, there was no sign of the skunk. He picked up the cushions from the floor and hurled them on the sofa. Then he heaved the sofa away from the wall. No skunk. He looked round the room, at the old stuffed chairs, at the table holding a coffee machine and at another, bare table. In the gloom he didn't notice the long, black drape behind the coffee table that concealed not a window, but an old fire exit door.

Mike thumped the sofa with the hockey stick. "It must have got away." He threw the stick across the room and left.

The young woman was waiting for him. "You're an asshole, Mike; a fucking asshole. And I never want to see you again."

His response was inaudible to Ciesta, who was quivering behind the curtain. She heard the front door slam. Now she couldn't get out of the building to relieve herself but she didn't care. She spent the night behind the curtain, pressed against the old door.

31

Herman was in the office the next day before the dean arrived. He greeted her with an apprehensive look, but she was too preoccupied with reissipating Ciesta to take much notice of him. However, no sooner had she sat down at her desk than he appeared before her and coughed. "Good morning, dean. I hope you are well."

"Very well, thank you, Herman." The dean began to sort through her In basket.

Herman was disconcerted; the dean seemed to have forgotten all about his arrest following the traffic havoc yesterday. "I wonder if I could talk to you about future experiments with my jammer."

"There will be no future experiments with the jammer, Herman. It has caused nothing but trouble. Surely yesterday was a lesson for you?"

"That was unfortunate, yes, but the jammer has great potential." Herman began to pull at his tee shirt, as he did when he was agitated.

"I'm sure it has," the dean said without looking up, "but I can't cope with any more crises this term." She stood up. "I have to go to the lab now. We can talk about this later." As she passed him to leave the office she said, "Herman, you are a whiz with electronics, for sure. But perhaps you could think of something less dramatic. How about an electronic fly that records conversations? Something like that." She didn't mention her plans for him if he did turn out to be a warlock; she wanted to be sure she was right first. She had to find out how to distinguish a warlock from other peculiar, gifted people. Did it require a blood test? She couldn't remember. Most warlocks are identified when they are children, she knew that, but she didn't know how you assess adults. She had never encountered the problem. In the meantime, she had to keep him busy.

"That's a brilliant idea, dean," Herman said. "I could use what I learned about the jammer. I'll show you my design when I've had time to make it." Herman left, clearly excited.

The dean entered the lab expecting to find Henrietta busy preparing a second counter-aff. Instead, Henrietta was marching up and down muttering, "Logos save me."

"What's wrong, Henrietta?"

"The Abraum salts haven't arrived. I phoned Express Packaging and they said they should be here by now." Henrietta looked at her watch. "It's well after 9:30. And, as you know, we only have until 10:30."

"Is everything else ready?"

"Yes. I took an alligator egg from the student lab. Chelsea will be coming to see you, by the way. She's furious that her study is delayed. I told her another would be here next week, but it was no use: she thinks she'll fail her comps."

"So as soon as the salts are here, you can proceed." The dean tried to sound calm. She had never seen Henrietta so agitated and thought that if she couldn't soothe her, Henrietta would screw up the concoction. "Let's review the items."

Henrietta pointed out the ingredients neatly laid out on a bench. "The egg's in the fridge."

"And we need the scales to weigh the salts, right?" the dean said.

"Oh, yes." Henrietta pulled out scales and placed them beside the ingredients. "My lebes is ready." She gave a deep sigh and smiled at the dean. "All set."

Just then Matilda bounced in. "Good morning, everyone." The dean had never seen her so perky. "I thought I would be present while Ciesta reissipates. We did go through this ordeal together, you know."

"We're waiting for the Abraum salts to arrive," Henrietta said. "Express Packaging said they should be here by now."

"I saw an Express Packaging man having coffee in Groundstones as I passed by," Matilda said.

"*What?* I'll have his guts for garters." The dean stormed out of the lab and slammed the door.

"What's the problem?" Matilda said. "Ciesta won't mind waiting a bit. What's a few more hours?"

"The problem is..." Henrietta resumed her marching back and forth. "The problem is, that if Ciesta is not reissipated by 10:30, she will exchange one human attribute for one skunk attribute every hour until she is a skunk forever."

Matilda sat down heavily on a stool. "Oh. Flutter the dovecotes."

"Exactly."

"What time is it now?" Matilda looked at her watch. "Almost ten. Do we know which attributes go first? Thank Logos we didn't know about this while we were skunks. It was bad enough trying to get back to campus without knowing there was a time limitation."

"No, we don't know which attributes go first."

Matilda got up to stare out of the window while Henrietta began to noisily sort metal equipment in a drawer. They were both startled when the dean rushed in carrying a small cardboard box. "I put a hex on the man," she said with satisfaction. "He'll never enjoy coffee again. It will always taste of anchovy."

"Oh thank Logos. Just in time," Henrietta said. "I'll go and get the egg while you open the box, dean."

"Got any scissors?"

Henrietta produced scissors and left for the kitchen. The dean attempted to pierce the plastic wrap around the box. "Aggh," she yelled with frustration. "Why is it we can never open anything these days?" She thumped the box on the bench.

"Deep breath, dean," Matilda said.

The dean remembered Adventitia's technique. She produced her talisperson and chanted:

This box is covered in plastic wrap
Undo it at once before I snap.

The plastic fell away and the dean was able to open the box and extract a bag of white salts as Henrietta emerged from the kitchen with the alligator egg.

"What's the time?" Henrietta asked.

"Forget the time, Henrietta. Concentrate only on concocting. Is there anything I can do?" the dean said.

"No thanks, dean." Henrietta weighed the salts, threw the ingredients into the lebes and chanted the same aff as before but omitting the last verse about the shortage of salts.

"Most impressive," Matilda said.

"What time is it now?" Henrietta said.

"10:30."

"Come on," the dean said. "Let's get it over there. Surely a few minutes can't make much of a difference."

"I'm afraid she will gain one skunk quality," Henrietta said. "Even with only a few minutes difference."

"I dread to think which skunk quality," Matilda said. "I hope it isn't the smell."

"Don't we all," the dean said.

Outside the Sorority Hall, Wanda and a skunk lay in the sun. They jumped up when they saw the trio with a lebes. Wanda ran into the hall and returned with a bowl and ladle.

"Relief at last, Ciesta," the dean said. "We'll soon have you back to normal."

The skunk licked at the contents of the bowl. The faculty waited in anticipation. As the dean was wondering what to do if this counter-aff didn't work, Ciesta appeared before them in human form. "Oh, bring on the dancing girls," she said and began to twirl around, wiggling her hips and waving her arms like a Hawaiian dancer.

"Welcome back, Ciesta," the dean said. She stared at Ciesta's body, wondering if she had a tail or hair or claws. No; but there was something different about her. Then she realised. "Have you lost weight?"

Ciesta stopped dancing and held out the waistband of her pants. "I believe I have. Wow. If becoming a skunk for a few days can achieve what Jenny Craig can't in six months, then it was worth it!" She began to dance again.

Matilda said, "You must be hungry. Why don't we all go to the Faculty Club for an early lunch?"

"Good idea." Ciesta ran ahead. "Come on." She turned to the others to urge them on like a small child does.

"She seems to have the energy of a skunk," Matilda said.

"No, skunks move very slowly," Henrietta said. "There must be something else."

"I think she's just happy to be herself again," the dean said. "She always was cheerful."

At the cafeteria in the Faculty Club, Matilda said to Ciesta, "I'll treat you to lunch. Or breakfast, if you wish. Would you like pancakes?"

"Yuck, no thanks. But I'm dying for some fruit." Ciesta placed a bowl of fresh fruit salad on her tray, thought for a moment and then added a Caesar salad.

"Is that all you want?" Matilda said. "Coffee? Some bread, perhaps?"

"No, thanks. This will be great." Ciesta waited for Matilda who paid for them both before they made their way to a table on the outdoor patio.

"You know what, dean?" Henrietta whispered. "I do believe the skunk attribute Ciesta has acquired is," Henrietta chuckled, "diet!"

"What do they eat?"

"Mice, lizards, frogs, and insects mostly."

"That's going to be difficult for her."

"Ah yes, but they also eat birds," Henrietta said. "So she can eat chicken and turkey and more exotic birds like pheasant, I suppose. And eggs. As well as fruit and raw vegetables, of course."

"Sounds like a healthy diet." The dean laughed. "Let's ask her what appeals to her."

After Ciesta had talked about her experience as a skunk for a while, and had related the incident of the previous evening, Henrietta said, "Ciesta, do you think being a skunk has changed your food preferences?"

"Funny you should ask that, Henrietta. I don't seem to want my usual diet. At least, not yet. I've never really enjoyed fruit before but this fruit salad is to die for." She took another mouthful.

"How about fish and chips? You used to love them."

"Yuck."

"Coca cola?"

"Yuck, yuck."

"What would you like for dinner tonight?" the dean said.

Ciesta thought for a while. "Chicken, maybe. With a salad. Why? What's the matter? What's so funny?"

The dean and Henrietta continued to laugh. "Good to have you back, Ciesta," the dean said.

After they left the Faculty Club, the dean told Henrietta she needed to talk—she wanted to discuss her idea of approaching a corporation for funds. "If I can get them to see the advantage of Mary Lou's brew, maybe even sell them a sample, they might recognise our value and give us some money."

"Hasn't Mary Lou quit?"

"Yes. Even if she has, we can still give them a taste of her brew. Where is it, by the way?"

"Locked up in the lab. At least the jars are."

"But we have her ingredients don't we? We could make some more."

"No, we can't, Aurelia. You can't sell her work. She owns the patent," Henrietta said firmly. "Anyway, I believe Mary Lou took the ingredients." The dean grimaced. She knew Henrietta was right. "The only thing we can do," Henrietta continued, "is persuade Mary Lou to return and ask her to donate the patent to the school. We can give her an award, or a scholarship or something."

Later that day, the dean settled into her chair, lit her hookah and inhaled deeply. She needed to relax and reflect. So many things had happened in the last few days but, at last, all was under control and the school could proceed normally. She had soothed the graduate student, the one who needed the alligator egg, by extending her deadline; her faculty were back to normal, although their theory that Ciesta's food preferences had changed to those of a skunk had yet to be confirmed, and even that would not be a disaster; the lab animals were back in their cages; Prunella had decided to leave on her own accord; Herman had been persuaded that his jammer was not a good idea and that he should concentrate on another project. She had yet to find out if her suspicion that he was a warlock was correct, but that could wait until she had consulted Circando.

The only problem now was to persuade Mary Lou to return. What irony; a few days ago she would have been delighted if Mary Lou had decided to leave. Now she needed her, not only to prepare more brew but to give the patent to the school. Contacting her parents was obviously the first action.

Yes, she thought, all is well and now I can look forward to the study of Gravity Quotients again and the arrival of the brand new servogadge. There's only another three weeks of term left. Surely nothing more can go wrong.

When the dean left her office she found a note from her secretary informing her that the Vice-President wished to see her.

32

Prunella had been working hard to plan her revenge on the dean. After searching the library shelves for a 'How To' book on Gravity Quotients she asked a librarian for help. The librarian pointed out a few theses on the subject. One of them, a Masters thesis, described a simple experiment with mouse hair and it also explained, with diagrams, how to set up a servogadge. Prunella made copies of the diagrams and the instructions.

The next step was to visit the lab while Henrietta was there. This was not difficult, as Henrietta spent more hours of the day in the lab than anywhere else. Henrietta greeted her with surprise. "Why Prunella, I don't often see you here."

"No, my research has always been in educational theory, which uses classrooms as labs. But now I'm interested in Gravity Quotients."

"Gravity Quotients? That's a very specialised field."

"Yes, I know. But while we were skunks, Octavia told us a story about the Great Griselda and how GQs were her area of expertise. I was so fascinated that now I want to know more." Prunella looked around the unfamiliar lab. "Matilda said there was a servogadge here."

"I believe we do have one stored away somewhere," Henrietta said. "It's pretty old and I've no idea if it works or not but I'll scope it out for you, if you like. I have to give a lecture right now but if you come back later…"

"Thanks, Henrietta. By the way, do you know of a Sophist called Berninda?"

"No one of that name here. Not while I've been here anyway," Henrietta said.

True to her word, Henrietta found the old servogadge and laid it out for Prunella. She was not there when Prunella returned to examine the equipment the first time, but the following evening she found Prunella fiddling with it.

"This is really hard to figure out," Prunella said.

"It's a very specialised field." Henrietta booted up the computer so she could analyse more traffic light data. "You should ask the dean for help," she said to Prunella. "She knows how that thing works."

The dean had one last assignment for her writing course, and that was to relate the most important event of the last three months. Well, she certainly had plenty to choose from, but on reflection most of them would give away the secrets of the school. She couldn't write about the faculty turning into skunks, nor the escape of the lirrypoops and mean mews, nor Herman's jammer, without explanations that no one would believe. She could write about giving her paper at MAST; hardly exciting, but at least it fit in with the popular concept of academic life. Or, she could write about the old lady at the police station as an example of human— what? Idiocy? Silliness? Folly?

She felt like writing about harassment of university Deans but she knew it would be a rant. Her last interview with the VP had been unpleasant, to say the least. He had told her that her school caused serious concern to the Board and that they had decided to give it a year's probation. If, at the end of a year, there was no increase in funds or research output, and if there was a single, even one more, embarrassing incident, the procedures necessary to close the school would be taken. "And you are not to admit any new students," he had said. "They will be unlikely to graduate."

The dean stared out at the pink building, now with the correctly worded shield in place. Should she approach the Otterbrooks? No, they were far too conservative. A major corporation was the best bet, one whose financial interests would benefit, one who turned a blind eye to ethical dilemmas. That should not be difficult to find, the dean thought.

A knock at the door interrupted her thoughts. "Mary Lou is here," the secretary announced.

The dean's spirits rose. "Show her in." Had the letter to Mary Lou's parents produced such a quick effect? No, they wouldn't have received it yet. She must be here on her own volition.

Mary Lou entered the office with a hang-dog look about her. "Good to see you, Mary Lou," the dean said. "Please sit down."

Mary Lou sat on a chair facing the dean and placed a small cage on the floor beside her. She looked up but didn't meet the dean's eyes, nor did she speak.

"Have you changed your mind about leaving?" the dean asked after a short silence.

"I've come to see if you'll have me back," Mary Lou said in a small voice.

"Is saucery no longer attractive?"

"It's not that," Mary Lou said. "When I got home my mother refused to have Marvin in the house. She said he smells, which he doesn't. And she said I'd stolen him and I have to bring him back. Which is true, I suppose. But he was condemned. You didn't want him anyway so it wasn't really stealing."

"I see." The dean saw her advantage. Obviously the lirrypoop was a major bargaining factor. She rubbed her chin. "Well Mary Lou, letting out the lab animals was a serious offence. It was you, wasn't it?"

Mary Lou nodded.

"On the other hand, you passed your exam with flying colours. It was unfortunate that your aff caused initial dissipation but it did turn out to have magical properties. So the faculty agreed to give you a special award. That should please your parents, yes?"

"Oh yes, yes it would," Mary Lou said. Her face brightened.

"We recognise your concern about animals," the dean continued, "so if you return to continue your studies you may concentrate on electronics. We have someone here who could tutor you. Would you like that?" Brilliant, she thought, that will keep Herman occupied too.

"Oh yes, I would," Mary Lou said.

"There is one condition." The dean leaned forward. "I would like you to donate the patent on your brew to the school. And be prepared to concoct on demand. Would you be willing to do that?"

"I had thought of going into business but I don't know enough about it."

"We would set up a contract where you would receive a small percentage of anything the school makes from it. Would that be agreeable?"

"That would be fine." Mary Lou hesitated. "Can I keep Marvin?"

"Certainly. We would have to find a place for you to keep it. NOT in your bedroom," the dean said. "And it—he—can't be in the faculty lab with the others. I shall have to think about it. You better leave it—him—here until I can think of a home for him."

The dean could barely conceal her delight as she ushered Mary Lou out. She must get the name of the person Adventitia knew in Prance and Gambol as soon as possible. Surely one taste of the brew should make them want to invest in the school. She could hardly wait. Needing to share her excitement, she hurried to the lab to talk to Henrietta.

"Ah, dean." Henrietta said. "Good. I was just going to call you. The new servogadge has arrived. There it is. I've dismantled my equipment so that bench is free." She pointed to where her traffic light experiment had been.

"Oh, I don't want to disrupt your experiment," the dean said.

"You're not. The aff is almost ready. But I have reached an impasse. I don't really want traffic lights to be red *all* the time, only when a driver is hurrying to make them. I can't get the formula right."

"Maybe you could hex the actual light," the dean suggested.

"I don't know, dean. I'll have to re-consider. Anyway, there's the box you've been waiting for. On that trolley."

The dean excitedly pushed the trolley over to the empty bench. "Before I unpack this, I've got some good news. Mary Lou showed up this morning. Her mother sent her back with the lirrypoop she took. Wouldn't have it in the house apparently."

"Does she want to come back?"

"I told her she wouldn't have to use animals. She can concentrate on electronics. She liked that idea." The dean patted the servogadge box. "Herman can tutor her. That should keep him out of mischief too. Oh, and she brought back the lirrypoop. I told her she could keep it but where, I don't know. She can't keep it here. She can't keep it in the student lab, so …"

"Why not?" Henrietta said.

"Then all the students will know about him—er, it."

"They'll get to know anyway. So why not be open about it?"

"Mmm. Maybe you're right. I'll think about it." Then she noticed the equipment on an adjacent bench. "Why, isn't that the old servogadge?"

"Yes," Henrietta said. "Prunella's been working with it."

"Prunella?"

"I was surprised too. I thought her interests lay in educational theory. But she wanted to set up the servogadge and experiment with it so I got it out for her."

"What does she want to do?" The dean was suspicious.

"I don't think she knows what she's doing quite frankly. Said she got interested in GQs after a story Octavia told them when they were skunks. Wanted to find a Sophist called Berninda."

The dean narrowed her eyes. "What did you say?"

"I told her there was no one of that name that I know of."

The dean forgot about Prunella in her excitement as she unpacked her new servogadge and set it up. Following instructions in the accompanying manual, she calibrated it. When she had finished, all the numerous small dials were set to zero and it was ready for use.

"I'm very rusty," the dean said. "I shall have to do some reading." She stroked the main body of the servogadge. "I don't want anyone touching this, Henrietta."

"Don't worry, Aurelia. No one has a clue how these things operate."

"I'm not sure I have either," the dean said. "There's been a lot of technical advances since my grad days. But the principles are the same, and the addition of a gyrometer will be a great help. It was so tedious to set that gauge by hand—it had to be exact or nothing worked."

"Can you bear to leave it and come for a drink?" Henrietta asked.

The dean put down the manual reluctantly. "Okay. I'll come back later."

Over a gin and tonic, the dean said, "I can't understand Prunella's sudden interest in Gravity Quotients. There's only about two more weeks left of the term and then she's leaving. For somewhere that values teaching." She raised her eyebrows.

"I don't want to cast aspersions," Henrietta said, "but I suspect she's up to no good. In fact, I think she had something to do with the disappearance of Octavia."

"She says someone doctored her fudge." The dean took a slow sip of her drink. "But I think she did it. Though how she managed to take some herself, I don't know."

"Why was she wearing Octavia's hat when she reissipated?"

"I've no idea," the dean said. "But I think we should keep an eye on Prunella. A strict eye."

The dean left Henrietta at the Faculty Club bar and returned to the lab to further explore the workings of the new servogadge. In the stairwell, she heard someone on the stairs above her. She stopped to look up and saw Prunella heading for the lab. "I don't want to be in the lab with her," she muttered, and turned around.

I wonder what Prunella's up to, the dean thought as she crossed campus again. I think a visit to her office would be in order. A master key gave her access to Prunella's office without having to go to the trouble of the door hex, and she switched on the light. Prunella had only just been about to enter the lab and, even if she was simply picking up something, the dean reckoned she had at least ten minutes to explore.

There was nothing unusual in the office except for a pile of library books on Gravity Quotients. If Prunella had made any notes, she must have them with her. The dean was about to leave when she noticed a small mirror on the bookshelf with a jar of moisturising cream and a hair brush beside it. She found an envelope in a drawer, carefully extracted a few hairs from the brush and placed them in the envelope. Just in case you try any tricks, the dean thought, and put the envelope in her pocket.

In the lab Prunella noticed the new piece of equipment but it did not register that it was a servogadge. She produced her drawings from the Masters thesis and continued to work through them on her servogadge. Now this dial registers the hair molybdenum ratio, she thought, and this one the Max Factor. What I really want is a hair. When I get it, it goes here. She pulled out a small bobbin like one from a sewing machine. I must wind the hair round this, counter-clockwise, and then the bobbin pushes in here. Now, if I find a hair, I don't really have to know the other settings; I can just put in the hair bobbin and twiddle the knobs until the dean rises. She cackled and sang:

Just a turn of my dials and the dean will orbit,
The dean will orbit, the dean will orbit,
Just a turn of my dials and the dean will orbit,
In the most uplifting way.

33

The dean lost no time in talking to Adventitia who said she would contact the Prance and Gambol representative she knew. "It's about this concoction a student made that affects the taste buds. You get to taste whatever food you think of no matter what you're eating. It's magical. You can be eating macaroni, think of leg of lamb, and that's what you taste!"

"Wow," Adventitia said. "Can I have some?"

"I'll courier you a jar." After all, the dean owed her for the servogadge.

A few days later, Herman remarked to the dean that he had seen a lot of Prunella lately. Had she? The dean had not noticed her, but over the next few days she became aware of her presence. It seemed that everywhere she went, Prunella popped up. She was there in the faculty lounge whenever she took a coffee break; she was there in her outer office on some pretext or other; she was even there when she went to the washroom. What is the woman up to, the dean wondered. Then light dawned: she's after one of my hairs and she doesn't know how to get one! She cackled to herself. Very well. I'll give her a helping hand.

The local pharmacy supplied a small hairbrush that the dean put in her pocket. The next time she saw Prunella in the washroom she pretended to brush her hair and then casually left the brush beside the mirror while she went to the toilet. When she emerged, the brush and Prunella had vanished.

Prunella was overjoyed—she had the dean's hair at last. She almost galloped to the lab, breathlessly removed the bobbin from the servogadge, carefully pulled off a single hair from the hairbrush, and wound it round the bobbin. For a moment she fumbled with the bobbin, which did not slip into place as usual. Take it easy, she told herself. She took a deep breath and tried the bobbin again. It went in easily.

Prunella let out a deep sigh of satisfaction. Now all she had to do was twiddle three knobs at random. She had been able to adjust the phi reading, the weight, and the molybdenum ratio, but she had no idea what the Max Factor was and there were a couple of dials that baffled her.

Like a radio operator, Prunella sat in front of the servogadge turning dials back and forth. She wondered where the dean was. She would like to be there when the dean left the ground so that she could triumphantly shout, "Up you go and may you regret that you ever messed with Prunella!"

At that moment the dean entered the lab, nodded to Prunella and turned to her own servogadge. I know, Prunella thought with a hidden smirk, I'll ask her to help me.

"Excuse me, dean. I'm trying to learn how to operate this servogadge but I'm uncertain what three dials are for. Could you explain?"

The dean moved over to the old servogadge and examined it. "What part do you not understand?"

Prunella pointed to the three dials. The dean turned two carefully. "What figure did you use for phi?"

"Phi is nineteen over four point two, isn't it?"

The dean didn't answer. She was working out a long equation on a piece of paper. Prunella stood on one leg and then on the other. Finally the dean said, "The Max Factor is 8.9. You turn that dial to 8.9 and then it should work. What are you trying to do, by the way?"

Prunella mumbled something the dean couldn't hear as she bent down to be on eye level with the dial. She turned it to eight, then eight point one and very slowly to eight point eight. She looked up at the dean and grinned. Eight point nine.

Prunella felt a sense of weightlessness at first and then light headedness. For a moment she thought she was flying, and when her head hit the ceiling, she realized she was. For a few minutes she hovered vertically but gradually her legs rose and she hung horizontally, like a body in a magician's show, with her face and toes pressed into the ceiling. She pushed the ceiling with both hands and managed to turn over so that she was looking down at the lab and the upturned face of the dean.

"My, my, Prunella," the dean said, "You do seem to have an uncanny knack of performing magic on yourself. First you eat your own doctored fudge and now this."

"How did this happen?" Prunella screamed. She kicked her legs and paddled her arms frantically but all she could do was drift across the ceiling. She clung to a strip light and tried to lower her legs but they refused to do anything other than float in the air.

"Weren't you trying to alter your Gravity Quotient?" the dean asked with a smile. "It looks like you succeeded."

"But it was your…" Prunella stopped.

"My hair? No, Prunella, it was yours. You stole my brush, yes, but it was your hair in it, not mine. I put it there."

Prunella continued to move like a swimmer. Then she stopped and looked down. "All right, dean, you win," she said through gritted teeth. "I've learned my lesson. Now, would you please let me down?"

"No way, Prunella. I warned you not to try and get back at experienced faculty, didn't I? You obviously did not listen. No, you are going to join another pain in the bolus—the Great Griselda. If she's still alive, that is." The dean chuckled. "Last time I heard, she was a peasant in the rice fields of China."

The dean moved across the lab and opened a window, wide. "Goodbye, Prunella."

As Prunella was drawn inexorably to the open window, the dean called out, "Tell Griselda that Berninda sends her regards."

Prunella clung desperately to the window frame but gradually her hands slid from it and she was off, floating like a child's balloon with the string released. With a gleeful smile the dean watched her drift out of sight before closing the window with a bang.

34

As the end of term approached, the dean sent for Mary Lou. "Mary Lou, I'm afraid you must delay your vacation. You are needed here for a few days to concoct quantities of your brew. I've got people from a big corporation coming next week. I'm hoping they will be so impressed that they'll fund our school."

Mary Lou shuffled and looked at her feet. "What's the matter?" the dean asked. "Did you have plans?"

"It's not that," Mary Lou mumbled.

"What then?"

Mary Lou wriggled on her chair before looking up. "Something happened when I was getting ready for my exam."

"Yes. Go on."

"I spilt one of my ingredients on the floor. The allspice."

"And?"

"I swept it up and used it." Mary Lou looked at the dean with despair on her face. "Don't you see? I don't really know what was in it. It could be anything that was on the floor. And that could have made the brew magical. Not what I did."

Oh Bloody Spell, the dean thought. Don't tell me. Just when I thought everything was under control. She stared at Mary Lou, who looked as if she was about to cry. "We don't know that, do we?" She thought for a moment. "We must experiment. Do you have any of the original allspice left?" Mary Lou nodded. "Then we need you to concoct two brews, one with the original and one with new allspice. Then we'll look at the two results."

She arranged to meet Mary Lou in the student lab the next day. "Henrietta's got all my ingredients," Mary Lou said. "Except the original allspice. I'll bring that."

"I'll arrange for Henrietta to be there," the dean said, "with the ingredients. And you go out and purchase more allspice, yes?"

"Yes, I'll do that," Mary Lou said. "By the way, where's Marvin?"

"Oh yes, I forgot. For the present he is in my stationery cupboard. Herman is looking after him. I think he will be better back with the others, during the vacation anyway. When you return you can keep him in the student lab."

"He won't get mixed up with the others?" Mary Lou said. "He won't be used? And then condemned?"

"No, Mary Lou. I'll make sure he's kept separately. But he needs to be there to be fed and cleaned. If he's by himself he might be neglected. Besides," the dean could hardly believe she was saying it, "he might get lonely on his own."

"That's true. I wish I could take him home but I can't, so he's better off here."

Because the student lab was full of students finishing experiments for their exams, and because the ingredients were in the faculty lab, Henrietta suggested they meet there. She pulled out Mary Lou's ingredients from a locked cupboard ready for the dean's and Mary Lou's arrival. Mary Lou brought her lebes, the old allspice, and some new allspice.

The dean explained why there were two types of allspice to Henrietta who glared at Mary Lou but said nothing. "So we need to make two concoctions, one for each allspice."

"I understand," Henrietta said. "Then we have to wait 48 hours before testing them. It was about 48 hours before the dissipation properties wore off, wasn't it?"

"Yes," the dean said. "But I still think we should be careful. Perhaps we should test it on a lirry before proceeding to taste it. Right, Mary Lou, get going."

Mary Lou fumbled so much hexing her lebes that Henrietta impatiently pulled out her talisperson and did it for her. Then Mary Lou, feeling foolish with Dean Virgo and Dr. Burghul watching her, repeated her performance. Once the brew had cooled a little, they all ladled it into jars and carefully marked them.

Mary Lou cleaned out her lebes and began again, this time with the new allspice. Once this brew was jarred and labelled, she relaxed. Until Dr. Burghul said, "Just a minute. I want to try something." She took the package of new all spice and dropped some on the floor. Then with a small brush she swept it into a new bag. "I want to find out if it's the energy required to raise the allspice off the floor that's the active ingredient."

"You mean you want me to do this again?" Mary Lou said. "I'm tired."

"Nonsense," the dean said. "Get going."

For the third time, Mary Lou danced round her lebes. The words, "Single, single, with my jingle," words she had chosen with such care, now mocked her. It occurred to her that she had agreed to do this for the school but now, after three turns, she wondered if she was up to it.

"Well done, Mary Lou," the dean said. "You will be a real expert by the time you've done this a few times."

"For sure." Mary Lou said.

Two days passed. During this time, Henrietta took the precaution of changing the code to enter the faculty lab to 5 6 7 8. It was not that she suspected Mary Lou of malignant intent, she just wanted to be sure. She also changed the code on the door to the lab animals. Unfortunately, she not only failed to inform other faculty, but she also forgot the code, leaving the animals unable to be fed or cleaned. The only person who could remedy this situation was the dean, who had to spend over two hours, in the middle of the night, altering the environcouls of the lab to undo the lock. She was not in the best of moods when she met with Henrietta and Mary Lou in the morning.

Henrietta silently laid out the three types of brew, some small spoons and a cage containing a lirrypoop. She knew the dean well enough to interpret the gleaming eyes, the taut mouth, the set of her shoulders, and to be careful. Not so, Mary Lou. Having completed her exams and seeing the end of term in sight she was bubbly and chipper. She had brought her lebes, just in case. This she placed on the floor before dancing around it chanting:

Bollocks, bollocks, time for frolics,
End of term, goodbye to pillocks.

The dean, with one hand on a bench and one hand on her hip said, "Mary Lou. What exactly are you doing?"

Henrietta seemed to be choking. With a muttered "glass of water" she entered the kitchen but left the door open.

Mary Lou stood still. She grinned at the dean and said, "Just expressing joy."

"Joy?" the dean bellowed. "If you can't be serious, you better leave."

Henrietta reappeared. "We are going to need Mary Lou to test the brews," she said evenly. "Unless you would like to do this at another time?"

"No. Let's get on with it." It occurred to the dean that Mary Lou had figured out her importance to the school and was now flaunting her power. No, she was too innocent, too naïve. The sooner they learnt how to concoct her brew themselves, the better.

As Henrietta discussed how to proceed with the tests of the brews, the dean calmed down. First they would test each of the three samples on a lirry. If the lirry did not disappear, Mary Lou would taste each sample. Henrietta wrote on the blackboard:

Sample A   Original allspice
Sample B   New allspice
Sample C   Swept-up new allspice.

"Right," Henrietta said, "Sample A." She took a small spoonful of the jam-like substance from a jar, opened the cage, and offered it to the lirry. After sniffing it for a second, a small pink tongue licked the spoon. The three people watched intently. The lirry licked again and then again in obvious delight.

"So far so good," Henrietta said. "It's not dissipated. Now for Sample B." She repeated the process. This time the lirry took one lick, but only one, and turned away from the proffered spoon. "Interesting," Henrietta said and opened a jar of Sample C. This time the lirry reacted as it had for Sample A.

"Well none have made the lirry dissipate so now we should try them. This is where you come in, Mary Lou."

"What do you mean?" Mary Lou said.

"We thought you should have the honour of being the first to taste," the dean said. "Seeing that it's your concoction."

"Oh, right," Mary Lou said. She picked up a spoon and licked at Sample A. There were the delicious tastes again as she thought of hot chocolate, sushi, ice-cream, and yam fries. "That works. I'm getting the tastes I think of. Now for Sample B."

This time Mary Lou did not react. All she could taste was something like plum chutney. "Nothing," she said. "Just tastes of chutney."

"Here, try the last one," Henrietta said.

Mary Lou stuck her spoon into a jar of Sample C. A seraphic look came over her face as the tastes of her imagination filled her mouth. "Ye-e-e-s," she said. "That works."

"How extraordinary," Henrietta said with a thoughtful look on her face. "So it must have something to do with the sweeping motion. Hmm. That's something to explore."

The dean was delighted. They weren't left with only a small bag of an essential ingredient as she had feared. Now they had a means of concocting as much brew as they wished and, furthermore, they did not need Mary Lou. At least there was that possibility. She and Henrietta must experiment, try to concoct the brew themselves and try out more swept-up allspice before reaching any conclusions. That was brilliant of Henrietta to think of sweeping some up. If it turned out that they could concoct at will, she must negotiate a release of patent with Mary Lou.

"It looks as if you can go on vacation after all, Mary Lou. Thank you for your help. If we need you again, I'll send for you. But we are now assured that your recipe can be repeated and we have enough to provide samples. And," she added, "you can stop worrying about spilling the allspice. In fact, if you hadn't done that your brew wouldn't be magical."

"Does that mean it wasn't something on the floor?" Mary Lou said. "So what was it?"

"Probably the energy that the sweeping motion gave to the allspice," Henrietta said. "I shall test it out. You may have discovered something very important. Well done!"

As Mary Lou picked up her lebes she turned to Henrietta and said, "You will look after Marvin, won't you?" Henrietta sighed. "Yes, I will look after Marvin."

Once Mary Lou was out of earshot, the dean said, "You better. That lirry is the only hold I have over Mary Lou. Though we may find we don't need her after all."

The dean left the lab feeling considerably more cheerful than when she had entered it. Now she could approach Prance and Gambol with confidence.

35

End of term brings relief to all university faculties, especially the end of spring term. A summer lies ahead with time to attend to one's own work, to write, and to catch up on reading. The dean of the Academy of Sophistry was no exception. She relaxed in her chair with her hookah to reflect on her meeting with Prance and Gambol. A deep inhalation filled her with contentment, a peace she felt was long overdue. This term had brought her nothing but strife but now the future of her school was assured, she could relax. Or almost assured; there were still the legal documents to complete.

P&G had sent two representatives, a man and a woman. The dean had explained the mission of her school, the goals of Sophistry, and the likely future of the graduates. The pair listened politely, but it wasn't until they were given a sample of Mary Lou's brew that they perked up.

"Wow," the woman said. "And you can make this? Enough to be marketable?"

They both retired to make urgent calls on their cell phones. When they returned, they told the dean that they wished to see more. The dean brought in Herman to demonstrate his jammer, outside, on a lawnmower, far from any other machinery. He told them he was working on an electronic recording fly that could be of use in board rooms and the like.

"These are just some of the projects we work on," the dean told the excited representatives. "We could do more, but unfortunately we are limited by the space the university provides us."

She took them on a tour of the Annexes, the shared lecture hall, and the lab. At the end the female rep could barely walk in her high heels. "You need a building," she said. "Where you are all together. You must walk miles a day."

The dean tried to look forlorn. "Exactly."

Reflecting on this meeting, and the subsequent positive talks with Prance and Gambol's CEO, brought a smile to her face, but not nearly the huge grin she wore as she remembered her meeting with the VP to seek planning permission for a new building. The thought of his face as he received the news of Prance and Gambol's intended endowment brought a joy that she had forgotten existed.

Now for uninterrupted hours in the lab experimenting with her servogadge, and for days at the lake writing her memoir on her new laptop. Another pull on the hookah and her imagination took off.

At the end of the summer, a tanned, relaxed dean returned to the university with new energy. She decided to ask Henrietta and Matilda for dinner so she could show them the preliminary plans for the Academy of Sophistry's new building. It even had a place for a coat of arms with the motto still to be decided. She had much to tell them about—all good. Prance and Gambol decided to invest heavily in the school, the VP had retracted his one year limitation, Octavia had decided to retire, Matilda had been promoted to full professor, and the dean had obtained a grant to compare the gravity quotients of chimpanzees with those of humans.

The dean held her head high as she shopped for ingredients for that evening's get-together. A barbecue would be nice, she thought as she considered steaks in the supermarket. While she was choosing three she heard uproar in the open spot near the meat counter. A crowd of people had gathered round a Prance and Gambol display table and judging by the oohs and aahs, they were enthralled by a product.

The dean pushed her way through the crowd to see what all the excitement was about. Arranged on the table was a stack of jars each labelled 'Mary Lou's Brew.'

At $45 a jar.

THE END